LIFE ... LUST ... LOVE

LIFE...LUST...LOVE

THE SHATTERING OF HEARTS

Stephen Paul Tolmie

authorHOUSE®

AuthorHouse™
1663 Liberty Drive
Bloomington, IN 47403
www.authorhouse.com
Phone: 1-800-839-8640

First published by AuthorHouse   10/14/2011

ISBN: 978-1-4634-4699-4 (sc)
ISBN: 978-1-4634-4698-7 (hc)
ISBN: 978-1-4634-4697-0 (ebk)

Library of Congress Control Number: 2011914181

Printed in the United States of America

Dedication

I dedicate this book to all those who have never found their
soul-mate in life or have like me, only ever found their one true love
and have lost them either to outside sources or to death.

As I write this book, I am still facing the everyday challenges of
looking for a special "someone" to bring me happiness, contentment
and a sense of belonging to someone who cares as much
about me as I care for them.

Life has a way of stripping away the non-essentials,
Until we are left with our real selves-
Unashamed before the world.
Refined by the experience; shaped by the things we've learned,
And the passion we've pursued, and finally
We know what we know;
And we love what we love;
And we still have the previous thing called "time".
And it's enough; it's more than enough.

. . . . Author unknown

In Appreciation

I express a heartfelt "thank you" to Yoram Snir for his knowledge, his talent and his artistic skills which he displays very well in the eye-catching cover for this book. I was fortunate to have his talent and his friendship at a time when I needed direction for my cover design.

Thank you Yoram, because the publication of this book would have been at a standstill without you in my corner.

Stephen Paul Tolmie

Acknowledgement

I express a sincere appreciation to Marion Broadfoot, a special friend, who contributed her skills in editing and in her time to read and type this manuscript. I also appreciate her expertise in the English language, which further contributed to the publication of this book.

Stephen Paul Tolmie

Life . . . Lust . . . Love
The Stattering of Hearts

By Stephen Paul Tolmie

When I was a young man at the age of six, I met someone very special. Miss Mills was my grade one teacher, a tall lady with long, shapely legs that accented her lovely frame. She had flowing brunette hair that surrounded her angelic face. Yes, my first impression of this lady was that I had been introduced to a goddess. It was her first year of teaching, having just graduated from teacher's college, and I was in her first group of students. Her challenge was to teach and make our little minds start to grasp the realities of the world and life's paths. It was her duty . . . yes, her occupation to have us search for knowledge, awareness, aspirations, and life's goals to obtain the passing report card. It would show that she had succeeded in passing on her knowledge and that her skills were indeed intact.

Unfortunately, as it turned out, this was not to be the case for either of us. I had no desire to concentrate on the studies at hand, but rather to dream childish thoughts of this lady, and just get caught up in the fantasy world of make believe.

My whole day was spent trying to have her spend special time with me; to have me as that one and only student, who was so demanding of her time. To this end I did succeed; but alas, this should not have been my goal. I would bring her apples, treats and roadside flowers . . . anything that would let me stand next to her, and drown myself in her presence. I would seek to walk her home, because I thought I was her knight in shining armour and she was my princess, to be protected from all outside factors.

As the year proceeded, this practice continued, and my educational accomplishments declined. It was a disastrous year for me to say the least and in some respects for her as well. My first year of school had been lost and my academic scores were far below acceptable; a repeat was indeed in order.

My "princess" a.k.a. teacher, was in tears as well. How had she not been able to reach this student? Was it her teaching skills? No as she thought, it was only this one pupil. She must have done something right, if all other students were to graduate to the next grade.

She realized that, due to her immaturity, she had not nipped this young lad's fantasy in the bud and pushed him to take a "hard-nosed" approach to the education process at hand.

In all honesty, it probably stemmed from the fact that this was her first teaching job and from the nervousness that accompanied her in trying to do the best possible job with a room full of young minds.

This lady did indeed go out of her way to let my parents know how sorry she was that she had not been able to reach me; to give me the drive to strive for that brass ring . . . better known as a passing grade in the further pursuit of educational knowledge.

On the other hand, I held no feelings of sorrow for the failure to pass on to another grade, but relished the thought of another year with this special lady.

Fate held a different approach for me, as she was transferred to a different school to teach, most likely at her request. For me, this was my first awareness that life was not always fair.

The new teacher for the following year was a young male teacher, and hence my learning skills were finally able kick in and a teacher fantasy was but a fleeting thought.

I continued throughout the elementary system, not being touched by flights of fancy, but rather enjoyed a steady climb upwards through the educational process. I returned to that young lad, doing childish things, but more reflective of my age. Life seemed simpler now, and I was content.

It was not until I had reached the eighth grade that I began seeing young ladies as something of interest and as a time to put aside my childish ways. The new problem now faced me. How did I approach the opposite sex? I was naive in the way about connecting to these girls, as most young boys are totally out of their element in these circumstances.

It was probably normal; but I was fumbling in my speech. Subjects of conversation of interest to them were totally unknown to me. How does one go about breaking the ice? Here I think I was like most boys of that age. I would watch them skip rope, play basketball, baseball, ride my bike around them in circles, and even sneak up behind them and scare them . . . anything to seek attention, and be in closer proximity to them.

I was in a school system, which at that time period, (the 1950's) the girls went in one doorway and the boys the other, never to be in close quarters with one another.

I always asked myself in later years if this was a throw-back to the Victorian era, and it probably was, since there seemed no other logical reason for this occurrence.

In that time period also, the school buildings were usually three to four stories in height, and therefore a fire escape chute was a mandatory piece of equipment that had to be attached to the building.

The children (one boy and one girl chosen at random) from grade eight were given potato sacks to go down the fire escape first, both to clean and then to open the doorways at the bottom. Having done this practice several times before, as it seemed to be almost a weekly occurrence, I could never figure out how the girls got to come out on one side and the boys on the other. I decided that I would take this curiosity of mine, to try and discover the answer.

On my way down the chute on the cleaning mission, I took it slowly, and felt the walls all the way down. I had always been instructed to lean to the right when going down, and discovered quickly, that half way down, there was a split in the chute, one to the left and one to the right; hence the two doorways. I had yelled up that I had completed the trip down the fire escape, and to send the rest of the pupils down. I also had walked back up the fire chute to the point of separation in the chute.

I leaned over to the girl's side and opened my legs for them to go through. You cannot imagine the blood curling screams that came out of the mouths of these young ladies. I did indeed make an impression on these girls (mission accomplished) and a strapping from the principal followed. I had sore hands, but now the girls looked at me some times oddly; but at least they were looking, and the ice had been broken.

The girl I had hoped to impress was indeed interested in this character, so my practical joke was not for nothing. I was still lost for words while in Vicki's company, but for some reason, talking on the phone to her, could often go on for several minutes every night. Both the parents seemed to go along with this practice, (this childish love if

3

you will) and it continued to the end of the school term. I was not too bright as to think to go to Vicki's home, only a few blocks away, or to ask her to go bike riding, or for a walk. In hindsight, I wish I was not so shy, or had the wherewithal to take the first step to make a connection with my real first love.

Fate again would raise its ugly head, and on graduation from public school to high school, Vicki chose one and I chose another school to go to.

From that time on to the very present, I regret that I had not been more vigilant in my quest, as she was lost to me forever.

The high school years here were also un-eventful. I would walk down the hallways trying to be friendly with the girls passing by. I would attend a noon hour dance, called a sock hop, at those times; but was afraid to ask a girl to dance. The girls that were usually dancing were dancing with one another, and it was a rarity rather than the norm, to see a boy and girl dancing together. It also seemed to be the girls of higher grades that were the ones participating in the noon hour dance. I was only in grade nine at this time. This noon hour dance seemed to disappear soon after I graduated from grade nine, whether it was from the lack of participation by the students, or that school work and assignments became more demanding and time became more crucial to their completion times.

There were occasional Friday night dances held at the high school gym. Here too, I was not the brightest guy on the block. The practice for the guys was to walk around in gym, while some of the girls were sitting on the benches above. Others were dancing, and trying to look cool. Occasionally, the guy would stop and try talking with the girl, to see if she would have a dance. Sometimes the guy was successful and other times not. I was not particularly a good dancer and had low esteem, so very often the whole night was spent just walking around and occasionally having a talk with a girl. This you would say was not too interesting a night's fun; but I did try and build up some nerve to ask this one and that one out for a dance. However, I usually left with a heavy head and rejection.

There never seemed to be any special bonding with any particular girl in the high school system. Graduation came, and the sixty-four dollar question was at hand. What was my future aspiration? What were my career goals? Was it work or more school? I am getting a little ahead of myself at this stage, so I must do a little back-peddling and fill in but yet another segment of my life.

Two of my best friends, both in elementary and high school and coincidently brothers, had always talked throughout our high school years about a graduation vacation together. They had said that it would probably be the last time of freedom for all three of us. Joining the work force or further education would soon be changing our lifestyles and having time for the three of us to get together would be difficult.

To this end we made a pact to save our vacation money and every other bit of money we could lay our hands on, to be able to do this great graduation vacation.

My best friends were from Holland and still had many relatives residing there, so they said we could probably live with some of their relatives for a short while, to help cut down on our actual expenses. My two best friend's names were Arend and Rudi and they said they would approach their parents on this whole vacation idea.

I was a usual guest at Arend and Rudi's home, so that talking with their parents was a comfortable, relaxing experience and not one that I was afraid to be involved in. Now the main topic of conversation would be about the three of us going to Holland and working out the details of its possibility.

My friend's parents were very laid back and being from Europe had a totally different outlook on life. The whole idea of us going to Holland didn't upset them and they were very approachable, listened well, and allowed each of us to express an opinion before speaking their minds.

The boys' mother and dad said they would be willing to write to their respective brothers and sisters to see if they would be willing to allow us to stay in their homes. Although they didn't say it directly to us, I have no doubt that they also asked their relatives to sort of keep an eye on us as well.

Once we heard back from the family members in Holland, we would then know more about our costs, when we could plan to go, where we would be staying, and what parts of Holland we would be seeing.

Arend and Rudi said that all European countries are so close that they would take me to different countries close by, and that I would be seeing a lot more of Europe than just Holland.

When I brought up the graduation vacation idea with my parents, my mother was thrilled, but my father was not as enthused, because I thought he was thinking it was going to cost him money. I explained the way it was going to be possible and explained as well that it all hinged on the response from Arend and Rudi's relatives in Holland. My mother convinced my dad that indeed it was a chance in a lifetime, especially with the boys' relatives helping out.

But for the moment it was just an idea. The favourable response was received from the boys' aunts and uncles and the dream was now a reality; our plans were set in motion.

The after-school jobs, gifts of money from birthdays and summer employment and our bank accounts were starting to grow, ever so slowly it seemed; but they were indeed growing. After four years of high school and with all of us passing, the timetable to go on our graduation trip was now at hand.

Because the boys had many relatives, they were going to split us up, in different homes, so as to not be a financial burden of having to accommodate all three of us in any one household. All the relatives that responded lived either in the same village or very close to one another. It would not be a problem for the three of us to together each day to plot out our day's activities.

The big day of departure was soon upon us, and after saying goodbyes to our parents at the airport, we were off to board the plane. My first travel experience was about to begin.

I had never flown before in my life, but the boys were old pros and so they knew what to expect. At this time, there still the existence of the old prop jet, and herein lay the problem. The plane was slow and we encountered a severe storm . . . just my luck! The plane would go up and down like a yoyo, depending on the flying conditions. We were either climbing upwards, where cold temperatures greeted us and we needed blankets to keep warm, or we were dropping quickly to avoid a weather situation. This all played havoc with my stomach, and for the thirteen hour flight, all I basically saw was a "vomit bag".

I was so happy to see mother earth that I actually got down on my hands and knees and kissed the ground. Oh my God! I did survive this ordeal!

I wasn't the best looking Canadian citizen to greet Arend and Rudi's relatives because I was totally green around the gills. All I wanted to do was to lie down and get my stomach to settle down and to sleep off the experience.

This I realized was not the best way in the world to start my stay with people I didn't know and was not sure how they would react to my poor greeting performance. Apparently everyone had a good laugh at my expense, although I was not told of this till long after the ordeal.

By the next day I was feeling my old self again and eager to start my adventures. However, I was forgetting my manners and didn't stop to realize that visiting with the boys' relatives was first and foremost, the importance for this day. Something that I had totally forgotten was that there would be a language barrier. I wouldn't know what was being said or even the topic of conversation. This was indeed a total learning experience, as I sat there and watched them laughing and enjoying the conversation at hand, totally unaware of what had been said or for that fact, why it was so funny. I would ask what was so funny, and somehow in the translation, the story lost some of its meaning; so I tried to have the appearance of being interested, although I was totally dumbfounded. I guess in hindsight, the experience would be something like a deaf person not knowing what is going on in the conversation, except that I could <u>hear</u>; but still didn't know what had been said.

The formalities were soon accomplished, and the three of us could now start exploring the freedom that Holland possessed. I was now at the ripe old age of nineteen years and what I was about to see really gave me a reality check. Holland, or for that matter, all of Europe had a totally different "open door policy" on things that were allowed and those that were not, things that weren't even thought of, in Canada.

I saw children going into liquor stores for their parents and purchasing alcohol. In Canada, the legal age for me to do this very thing was twenty-one years of age. How progressive this country and standards seemed to be.

I saw government controlled buildings where you could sign yourself in and under a doctor's control, you could experiment with drugs. You would however, not be allowed to leave until the doctor authorized your departure. Arend and Rudi's uncle took the three of us to "section seven" in Amsterdam, where ladies walked openly nude or sat in their windows displaying themselves and offered you sex for money. There were women there of every age, body type, and nationality for you to choose. I later found out why it was called "section seven". As it turned out, there were seven solid blocks of townhouses of ladies from which to choose.

There I was with my face pressed against the window. I would have been happy to spend all my time and money at this location. The boys said that we could only spend a little while here as there was more to see and do. Possibly we might be able to return for another experience with these ladies. For the life of me I could not imagine how it could ever get any better than this moment, so reluctantly I left.

God knows how I wished we had this type of service back home, as it would probably save a lot of marriages. If a man could have this kind of service and afterwards, go home to his wife, who was either too tired or not interested in having sex then both the man and the wife could be happy. He could enjoy sex and she wouldn't have to "perform". It could be a marriage of contentment for both of them because they would both have their wishes fulfilled.

There are many other advantages to these ladies and this type of service, but are too numerous to mention. I will leave it up to you to draw your own conclusions.

One of Arend and Rudi's aunt's homes, that I was to stay at for awhile, had four mature children who still all lived at home. There were two boys and two girls. Since the older boy was away on a business trip, I was to have his room for the period of my stay. Fortunately for me, this family was chosen as they spoke a little English and were eager to polish up their English skills.

It seemed strange at the beginning . . . new home environment, new family members, new foods, and preparation methods. I was always trying to put my best foot forward, with manners, clean language and trying to be the best guest in their home that I could be. At different times through meal times and afterwards, conversation quite regularly went back to the Dutch language, as obviously they were more comfortable with it.

They could express their message to other family members directly. I sensed it would be a difficult job to find the correct English word; plus it was just natural to speak your native tongue.

During these times, I felt a little homesick, because I was lost to the conversation happening at times and was missing being involved in a regular daily discussion, about matters that affected the family . . . or directly me. I felt like a bump on a log; I was totally out of sorts and felt very alone.

The family was very kind and once they realized that I did not understand the conversation, would start again speaking some English and Dutch sentences to me, to make me feel part of the topic at hand.

The one daughter caught my eye, as she had natural beauty without the need of makeup. She somehow seemed to have a glow about her, and I wanted to show her that I was attracted to her.

Her name was Yannie and one evening she stayed behind and joined in on the conversation after the meal was done. The family members slowly drifted away to bed and we were soon alone on the couch, just talking with some English and Dutch sentences, desperately trying to understand each other's comments and meanings.

I found out that she was a mother's helper . . . much like a "nanny" in Canada . . . where she would go and stay in that person's home for the day and each day after that, till the person had recovered from surgery or from having a baby, as examples. Yannie would do all that was needed in running the home environment.

We talked, although with some difficulty, about everything under the sun that we both were interested in, or that we wanted to know about the other person. For the first time of my stay in this family's home, I felt like part of the family. We had said our good nights and each of us headed off to our separate bedrooms.

I was laying there in bed thinking what a great night I had just had, and was drifting off to sleep, when I sensed the doorway opening. A chill momentarily grasped its hold on me. What was going on? Seconds later the bedding was being pulled back and a warm body was now beside me. I wondered if the older brother just returned from his business trip and not wanting to disturb me, just climbed into the bed. I nervously turned over, not sure who I would be greeting.

But to my surprise and delight, it was Yannie. She quickly put her hand over my mouth, as her parent's bedroom adjoined mine, and she didn't want me to be startled and ruin the moment. Her lips were now on mine . . . a long passionate kiss, as her hands stroked over my body. The fireworks were going off in my head, as my hands were now exploring her very delightful body and the pleasures that lay ahead. We were restricted in making love not from the pleasure we were both

9

experiencing; but from making too much noise, so we would not wake the parents on the other side of the wall. Yannie and I held each other after making love, each feeling a bond of closeness and a strong desire to taste once again the pleasure of each other's body, which we did throughout the night.

Soon, the morning light was sneaking through the lower part of the window which the blind did not quite reach. Yannie was leaping out of the bed, because her work day was approaching, and her parents would be soon getting up to start the day's activities.

When I came down to breakfast that morning, I was a little scared about my morning greeting. It did not take too long to realize that our love-making had not been heard by her parents and that all was well in my world.

The boys and I did some activities together, going to Paris, France for the day and taking in the typical tourist sites and enjoying our time. Somehow I could not get over the feeling that I was really looking forward to being with Yannie, rather than just spending time with the boys. It was very difficult that night at the supper table, sitting across from Yannie, listening as the family spoke mostly in Dutch about the day's events. It didn't seem to matter that I was not included in the conversation, as I was looking forward to the after meal timetable of family togetherness. I was also being hopeful that Yannie and I would be alone on the couch for the balance of the evening as well.

As fate would have it, we were indeed alone that evening; but somehow I sensed that her parents had a feeling about our new relationship and chose to allow us to have this special time alone.

We did make love again that evening, and throughout the night. It was even more emotional, with more feeling. A bond of closeness was definitely forming. I was feeling a sense of oneness with this lady. The next morning at breakfast, her parents seemed somehow different. Even now her parents were feeling more like a part of my life and there too, a bond of closeness was forming.

I told the boys about my feelings for Yannie and how my nights would be occupied with her. The days seemed to fly by, waiting for my time with her. We spoke of a life together, the love that was bonding each of us together and where the future might take us.

Yannie bought me a dictionary that would convert words from Dutch to English meanings as we promised to write to each other after my departure to Canada. The balance of my stay with Yannie only reinforced our feelings for one another.

Time stands still for no one and suddenly our last night together was here. Tomorrow I would be on my way back home to Canada. We spent the evening in each other's arms, making love for the last time, and pledging our love for one another and for a future together.

All too soon, the morning was upon us and the trip to the airport had arrived. One last final kiss, a final goodbye, a last hug, lots of tears and the boys and I were off to the loading zone at the airport.

In my defence, when I arrived back in Canada, I did try to write to Yannie. In fact I made several attempts at composing a letter. I found it very difficult to find the right words in Dutch, to give the meaning to what I was trying to express in English. Yannie knew some simple phrases, some simple everyday words; but she was not in any way fluent in the English language.

I started to doubt myself, my love for her; I started to question myself. Was this really what I wanted in life? I asked myself what my expectations from this relationship really meant to me. Did I think it would work? If I moved her to Canada and we started a relationship, there was a strong language barrier. How would we get along on a daily basis? Again I asked myself if I really loved her, or was it just the fact that this was lust and she was there for the taking. Was I caught up in the moment? All this conflict within me ground me down.

I was too young; I was not as ready as I thought I was, for a life time commitment. I decided I had to LET IT GO!!

Once again in hindsight, I periodically think of this lady and how I let the potential happiness of love and a bond that did seem real, slip away from me. This was all because of my lack of maturity and willingness to put some serious thought into actually trying to make it work.

I let this loss of love, happiness and a good life SLIP THROUGH MY HANDS. This would seem to be the practice throughout my life!

Another piece of my life explained, and yet another chapter to begin the next phase and the pursuit of love and the ever evasive happiness that I had always hoped for. Yet when it did and does present itself, I am not able to recognize it.

My mother was talking with a church elder, who also happened to be a dean at Fanshawe College, and he told her of a good course that would be starting in September and thought it would be of interest for me to check out.

I did this and soon, another two years of College education lay ahead of me. This was an interesting course, and for the first time I could see a future in my life. I was no longer on a dead end road. This course offered a summer job and a full time job on completion. How great is that? I continued my usual shy ways with girls, sitting in the hallway, talking with this one and that one; but no special bond was ever formed. The first year of the course was complete and summer employment was about to begin. Three of us were sent to Sault Ste. Marie to work in the office up there. We were to go to Saint Joseph Island, to record information about the residents there and to live among them. This island seemed a bit remote, since the only way to get from the mainland to the island was by ferry and we had to conform to the structured times of arrival and departure.

This was to be a great adventure; although we were instructed not to visit the only two bars on the island, but to drink among ourselves. *We were not to get too friendly with the residents* was the official command. This seemed like a reasonable request, but was short lived. The weather for that time of year was still cool at night, and since we were living in a cottage, we were cold when we went to bed. So we went looking for some firewood for our fireplace. We had not driven far, when we discovered several small piles of firewood, already cut and stacked along the side of the road. We thought this was fantastic, a ready supply, and there for the taking.

Boy, were we wrong! It was apparently the practice of the residents on the island to do this, so that they would have a ready supply for their own fireplaces, to use during the winter months to supplement their propane gas costs during the winter. The police were called and we were hauled into our boss' office on the mainland for a stern warning, and to be more aware of island procedures and practices in the future.

The end of summer was drawing near, and as we mingled among the residents, it became clear that we would be leaving soon. A few of the younger residents suggested we have a going away party, and we went along with that idea. Unfortunately the word went around and a huge number of people started to show up, to the point of overflowing. There were bodies everywhere you looked. People were found throughout the house and the yard was full of party animals.

Here is where my story begins. I had gone upstairs to use the bathroom, and was doing my thing, when the door opened and Brenda came through the doorway. She was pretty well intoxicated, and as I tried to assist her, she began to disrobe me. Being a gentleman, I liked what she was doing, so allowed her to continue. It was not long till we were on the floor making love, when again the doorway opened, and a group of people stood there staring at the action.

The rest of the night we were the topic of conversation . . . even into the next day. The day after that, we were on our way home; summer was now over, and it would be soon back to school to complete the second year of the course.

As I think back, I was 20 years old, and had finally had sex again. It had been a long, dry spell. The days of Holland and that special lady Yannie, were only distant memories. I was more determined to find a relationship and start a long term commitment, hopefully finding a girl at Fanshawe College.

The second year of the course had now commenced, and even though I had strong desires to find a girlfriend, all that happened was that I retreated into my shell of shyness, and merely watched the girls go by, afraid to make that contact. However, I wished with all my heart, that I could find that specific someone to fill my lonely spirit.

Graduation day came and went, and a full time job was now the order of the day. As I had said earlier, a job offer came with this course, so there was no difficulty in procuring that. It was just "who" had made the offer for the position that was the unknown.

I was offered a job in Middlesex County, in the village of Arva. This was a fair distance from my home in the village of Union, a good hour's drive there and back. As with any first time job placement, I was young and naive, and the usual office pranks were played on me. The months rolled on and I was soon becoming comfortable with my job and the steady learning skills were developing to the point, that I was becoming an asset to the company. I was so pleased when I was taken into the boss' office and told that my six month job evaluation was very satisfactory and to keep up the good work.

Having a job was fantastic, but all work and no play, was still leaving Paul unfulfilled. I did the usual weekend thing with my buddies; but the evenings still left me without someone to call for a date. I was told of a bar, called the John Scott Tavern, where nursing students hung out. Thursday night, was also when the OPP students attended. So it was a very busy bar and you had to get there early, or you couldn't get in. There was an old saying . . . *if you needed a date, get a nurse.* It was a common saying among all the guys in St. Thomas. Being still very shy, I did not go to the nurses' residence, to inquire if there was a girl who wanted a date; but rather I hung out at the bar, hoping for a special encounter, but it never came.

The nurses were having a fund raising car wash, to help pay for their graduation party; so the local service station was very busy, with a steady flow of cars to wash and money to be made for their party. It was at this car wash that I met Kim. We seemed to hit it off right from the start. I was impressed with myself. I actually had the nerve to ask her out on a date, and she accepted. It was like the "Fourth of July" fireworks, inside my head. I was finally going to have a girlfriend; life seemed rich and full, for the first time.

The graduation day was not too far in the distant future, so my timing had been perfect, and the invitation to her graduation ball soon followed. We became a couple, enjoying all the usual activities that came with dating,

The sex was fantastic and often, and I was elated. My life seemed to finally be coming together; there seemed a path of happiness that I was going to go down. Life's flow seemed like a land of milk and honey, total contentment and purpose.

We had found one another, and soon we were engaged to be married. It was a regular routine kind of time for us, visiting her parents in Chatham, mine in Union. Everything seemed to be as it should, when two families were happy with the union of their children.

Kim asked to borrow my car to go back to Chatham one specific weekend to be with her friends. Of course, I thought she was going to start looking for her bride's dress with her sister and mother. When she returned Sunday night, all did not seem right. She was very distant, almost withdrawn. I was not seemingly allowed into her world.

Kim had asked me to give her some space, and I readily complied with her wishes. Was it just a bit of fear of marriage, of a commitment to one another, family pressure, and the whole idea of planning for a wedding? These are the thoughts that were going through my head. Never in my wildest dreams was I prepared for what was to happen.

When Kim and I finally got together for a coffee and our talk, she still seemed uneasy with my company. *What was wrong? Was there a problem in our relationship at this point for some reason?* Kim told me, that there was no easy way to say what she had to say. Yes, there was a problem. She was pregnant; but NOT by me.

You could have blown me over with a feather. I was momentarily in a state of shock. I stammered, *"By whom? When have you been unfaithful?"* Kim explained that it was a previous boyfriend, and they had just broken up the week before I met her at the car wash.

Kim told me that the boyfriend, when informed of her pregnancy, did not want anything to do with her ever again. She was so scared of the pregnancy. What would her family think; what would my family think? What would be going through my head, when she wanted time to be alone, to come to grips with the situation?

I told her that I loved her very much, and I would accept this child she would be having as my own. I still wanted to marry her and spend my life with her. Kim asked for some time, to have some space, to deal with her thoughts. I agreed to those terms and would wait for her to call me when she was ready. During that month long period of silence, my life was put on hold; my mental state was almost in total collapse. I feared the final outcome, as my mind began playing games back and forth.

Kim finally called, and told me she had been in contact with the previous boyfriend, and that he had a change of heart, and indeed wanted her and the baby. She would be returning to Chatham, to begin her life with him.

I was devastated! My world had collapsed. The lady that I had thought was to be a big part of my world, had now vanished. No further contact would be happening. I was totally unprepared for these new circumstances. I withdrew from the world of happiness; only to go into a world of everyday just existing, doing just what was required of me, and returning to that state of a shattered heart, the future looking bleak.

Once again I was alone, and many months of unhappiness and sorrow would now be my company. *LIFE was the pits*!

Once again, a friend of mine took me under his wing, so to speak, and told me to meet him at the bar that the student nurses frequented on Thursday nights. I was a bit reluctant at first, and then decided that it was time to finally get out and rejoin the world. Upon arrival at the bar, Barry met me at the doorway, and told me to follow him to his table. I was surprised as I walked towards his table because it was full of people I knew, and yes there were several student nurses sitting there as well.

The band was playing great tunes from the late 50's and I surprised myself and asked one of the student nurses to dance. I felt a transition come over me, from one of sadness to a spirit of happiness, as we danced on. The night was a total change in attitude for me; I was enjoying myself for the first time in a long time. I asked the student nurse her name as I escorted her back to the table. Her name was Erin and she was in her first year of nursing at Elgin General Hospital. I asked to drive her home, but she said that she had come with a carload of other nurses, and wanted to return home with them.

At first I thought that I had been totally turned down. Then as she was leaving she asked if I would be there next Thursday night and she was gone. I had obviously made a good impression throughout the evening, and I patted myself on the back and said *"You still got it kid"*. The days seemed to drag on, as though Thursday would never appear. I was high on expectation, and wondered if Erin in fact would be there? My question was quickly answered when I accidentally bumped into her chair, as I was looking around and not paying too much attention to where I was going. She smiled up at me and asked me to sit down with her.

Someone at the table said *"You're just in time to buy the next round"*. Lucky me; but I did oblige. I was ticked off at the thought that I was stuck for such a large bill; but wanted to make a good first impression. So I quickly did not let the situation get the best of me. Erin and I laughed, danced, and talked through out the evening, and we seemed to be forming a tighter bond with one another. That evening, Erin did in fact let me drive her back to the nurse's residence, and we discussed getting together soon.

Erin said she was going home that weekend, but for sure we would see each other the following Thursday night. I gave her my phone number as a precaution that she may not appear, and I really did not want to go to the bar if she was not going. I was totally surprised on Friday night when Erin called and said her sister Stephanie could not get her car going. Would I drive her to London? I answered in a heartbeat, that I would be pleased to take her. I picked Erin up within the hour, and soon we were on our way to London. It actually was great to spend more time with her so soon, and a better chance to get to ask questions and learn more about her. I was not ready for the next step.

Erin told me to come into her home, and lo and behold, her mom and dad greeted us at the doorway. Her dad said *"Come on in son and try some of my home-made wine"*. Erin told me that it was very strong and to only have one glass. Erin was right, it was high octane stuff, and I quickly was feeling its affects. I was not sure what the alcohol level was, but it was obviously very high.

I parted company soon after the drink of wine, but not before a kiss of appreciation was delivered by Erin. I asked if she would like to go to the show Saturday night, and she agreed. On my way home I thought how quickly I seemed to be getting into a potential relationship. I had already met the parents, so that hurdle was over with. I must have passed inspection, since we were on for the next night. Erin and I went to the show, and out for drinks afterward. I asked if I could come over on Sunday to drive her back to St Thomas, to the nurse's residence. Erin's mother said *"If that's the case, you might as well come for lunch"*. Boy was I shocked at how quickly I seemed to be moving into the family tree.

From that point on, Erin and I became a couple and we were building a lasting relationship. After graduation, Erin went back to London to a job at the hospital there, and I still resided in the city of St. Thomas. We were still dating on the weekends; but now it seemed totally different. Instead of us going out, it became the group that was going out on the weekends. It was the "dirty dozen". There were Erin's roommates, her sister, her room mates' brothers and sisters, and a few friends thrown in for good measure. From that point onward, we never had a separate date and Erin would not even consider just the two of us going out. Erin's words to me, *"If you don't like it; then don't come over on the weekends"*.

I was totally dumbfounded at her new attitude but like a fool, I went along with Erin's wishes. I was hopeful that this was just a stage; that the novelty would wear off; that this was a phase of rekindling the friendships lost when she was away in St. Thomas at nursing school. I was desperate (stupid) for a relationship and this had been the closest to one in a long time. So I played along. Erin seemed to become more and more involved with this group of people, through basketball teams, baseball teams, out partying . . . whether it was house parties or bars, or generally not including me in her life.

I told her that I was not happy with the way our relationship was going and she just smiled and said nothing. How do I reach her? What was I doing wrong? How do I get the relationship back that we had? These were questions that were racing through my head on my return trip home. I had finally come to the realization that it was going to be her way or the highway. I had to decide.

I foolishly gave up my self esteem, my manhood, my ability to have self respect, all in the name of desperately wanting a relationship, of being close to another soul. What was I doing to myself? At least, whatever happened, I would have no one to blame but me.

To say that I was a fool would be the ultimate understatement of all time. I wasted many an hour rethinking my past actions and I still cannot believe that I let this person control me, to the point that I was like a dog . . . to come when I was summoned.

This craziness was to continue for 19 years. Time was going fast, and I was at a stand-still existence. I was not happy, not looking forward to anything, except a phone call that she had time for me. I would then be allowed to hang out with the group, not even have quality time with her. I was still residing at home, saving up for a down payment on a home of my own.

My thought was that I would then have something to offer Erin and our relationship would/might resume. It is funny how one's mind plays games, a total denial of reality.

One day, my father asked me to paint the front and rear porches of our home, and as I obviously had time on my hand I complied. I had started on the rear wooden porch. It was a massive structure. In those days, large porches were the "in" thing to have. I had done a small section of the deck when I sensed somebody was watching me. As I turned around, there was the new neighbour lady from two doors down. She had heard the radio playing, and my awful singing, and came to check out the sounds.

We introduced ourselves and she asked if I would like her to stay and keep me company. I was more than anxious to comply. The company was very welcome because the job was very boring. We talked about a variety of topics, and then got into a little more personal information. Emily was her name, and she had a husband and two children.

Her mother-in-law Nell lived with them. Nell's husband had recently died and she had money to help Emily and her husband Ken with the down payment on the house. Emily told me that Ken was a very busy union representative and she felt abandoned regularly, due to his busy work schedule. She said that Ken was not too attentive and she felt unloved, and that their marriage was very rocky. I could not believe that this lady was confiding all this personal information about her life.

I was feeling a little uneasy learning all these facts. Emily reached up and grabbed the railing and started to pull herself up the staircase. I yelled *"Emily, stop! I think that the railing is still wet."* She looked at her hands and wrists, and indeed they had grey paint all over them. I told her that I had some paint thinner down in the basement, and would go down and bring it up to clean off her hands.

I was surprised as I turned to the climb up the stairs and there stood Emily. She said *"I thought I would come down to save you some steps".* I just smiled and proceeded to undo the top on the paint thinner, dabbed some on a clean cloth, and approached Emily's outstretched hands.

I gently applied the cloth to one hand with small circular movements, and was surprised when she started to stroke my face with her other hand. Our eyes met; then our lips touched, and we were in a full embrace.

My father had made a rough recreation room in the basement. He had painted the floor and walls, and added two second-hand couches, some small tables and lamps, as a retreat area for me to have some private space away from my parents.

Emily and I proceeded towards one of the couches, still embracing, stroking one another's body, feeling the strong desire to make love. The light was turned out and the couch was in motion as our bodies rocked. We made love several times that afternoon, and were just laying there after our last love making session, when I heard the front door open upstairs.

Emily and I scrambled to get our clothes on and make ourselves presentable and had just enough time to turn on the lights, when my parents started to come down the stairs. They had been out of town for the day, visiting relatives. It was now almost the supper hour and they had been anxious to get home, and my dad probably wanted to check on my painting progress.

I believe that they were both in a state of shock. A mature lady they did not know was in their basement with their son. I quickly started to introduce Emily to my parents and told them that she had just moved in two doors down. I explained that she had been talking with the neighbour lady next door while she was out hanging up her laundry, and had spotted me.

Naturally, when Doris went into her house, Emily wanted to meet me. She had come over to do that very thing when she had grabbed the railing which was wet. I was being polite and cleaning the paint off. I told my parents that it had just happened, moments before their arrival home. We were just heading upstairs as they arrived.

I do not know to this day if they believed me or not. I thought that I had composed a very believable story in such a short moment, and who would question that it was not true. Emily left and my father told me that I was very slow at painting the deck and that I had better get cracking. He said *"At this pace you won't finish the job in weeks"*.

I told him another tall tale of how I was just trying to do a good job. Unfortunately he did see through this comment, and said *"Cut the crap and get the paint job done, today"*! I could not believe how fantastic the day had been. I had had unbelievable sex with a total stranger. Even more remarkable was that I had seemingly gotten away with only Emily and me knowing that it taken place.

I was now like a kid in the candy store. I wanted more of this pleasure, the act of two bodies been intertwined. I looked for every opportunity to get her alone, to ask when we could make love again; but it seemingly was very difficult and leaning towards impossible for it to happen.

There was her mother-in-law, kids or husband on her side, and my parents, my job, or other duties assigned to me by my parents that infringed on the opportunity for any connection. When our eyes would meet, there was a momentary connection, but it soon fled away, not to get caught in the act.

I thought to myself that where there is a will, there had to be a way. I started to study Emily's everyday routine. Where did there seem to be free time for Emily and me to connect?

It didn't take long to become evident where the free time availed itself. Emily and Ken had a Volkswagen for their transportation. Thank God for the noisy vehicle. It was as if an alarm clock would go off every morning, as Emily took her husband to work. My bedroom was at the front of the home; so all I had to do was note the time they left and when Emily returned home.

Once a regular time pattern showed itself, then my next hurdle was to get out of the house at that hour of the morning, without my mother, who was a light sleeper and had ears like an owl, hearing me leave.

Again, I had to do some more planning, looking for a possible solution to this particular barrier, that was standing in my way of connecting to Emily in the morning.

The driveway of our home would only hold one car, and since there was no parking on the street overnight, I had to find a different location to park my car. The solution to my problem was lying right at my feet, and I did not recognize it. They say that you can't see the forest for the trees, when looking for a problem solution. I believe that was my case.

The mind starting spinning, looking for all or any reasonable, explainable, or logical reason why I would be leaving the house so early in the morning, because I did not go to work for a couple of hours after Emily had returned home.

Finally, the solution was at hand. I even believed it myself and so I told my parents that I was going down to get my car early in the morning. I wanted to make sure that it was running fine, and it would be close at hand when I needed to go to work. The other reason I gave was that I enjoyed a brisk walk in the morning, just to ease into the day. Afterwards, I thought to myself that I may have over-killed the reason with so many explanations; but it seemed that the story passed with flying colors

And so, the next week the plan was to go into effect . . . its trial run. I was shocked at the sound of the Volkswagen motor roaring on Monday morning. It was indeed an early rise for me, but hopefully a successful reunion was at hand. Emily was surprised when she first arrived home to see me standing in front of their home, waiting to greet her. The first morning we discussed what was happening and what we were doing. This was so risky, a lot to lose. Emily gave me a kiss, and then she was gone, into their home.

The plan had worked, but not as I had hoped. Although I did not know what the plan of action was after we made our morning connection. I was deep in thought as I walked down the street to where my car was parked at the corner gas station. Had I made a fool of myself? Was the previous love-making session a one time deal? Was it just that Emily was in the mood for love and I was available, and naive of the ways of women? I drove my car back home, and went back to bed. When I went downstairs, my mother said *"I thought you were going for a morning walk to ease into the day. What happened"*?

Boy, I was caught in my so-called well-thought-out reasons for my new morning activity. I quickly said *"It is the first day of the new routine, and I will have to ease into that, before I ease in the day"*. This seemed reasonable, and so my mother let it drop. I had gotten away with it, but guess what; it now had to continue, for a little while, even if Emily was not going to meet with me in the morning.

The next day, I was up at the roar of the Volkswagen engine; but this time I walked down the street to where my car was parked, got in and drove it slowly back to my home. I sat and listened to the radio, all the while contemplating what I would do when Emily returned home. I told myself, that when she arrived home, I would just ease out of the car at the same time, greet her and see what would happen from then on.

My wait seemed an eternity, or possibly it was just second guessing myself about what would happen, could happen and might happen. It would all be decided in a very few minutes. Emily arrived home and apparently was not aware that I was in the car. As she got out of her car and started to head towards her home, I got out of my car, and said in a loud voice *"Good morning Emily"*.

She stopped dead in her tracks, and turned quickly towards me. *"Good morning Paul"* she replied. *"Are you in a hurry this morning? You already have your car parked in front of your house."* My mind tumbled in search for a quick, reasonable response to her question. *"No"*, I said, *"I was just thinking of going for a walk, to ease into the day"*.

I could not believe that I had said that! The very line I had told my parents about my change in routine had just come out of my lips to Emily. She smiled and said *"If I was dressed, I would go for a walk with you"*. She could see my puzzled look, and proceeded to open her coat. All she had on was a sheer white nightie under her coat. I could not get the full impact of her body outline, as it was early morning, the distance from me, and the quickness of the exposure.

From our previous love-making session, my mind recalled the vision of beauty and for a brief instant I was lost in the moment. I quickly realized that she was starting again towards her front door, when out I blurted *"I could wait for you, if you wish"*. Emily said *"Why don't you just come inside with me now"*.

It was as though I was an Olympic runner, because in a heartbeat I was standing there beside her. Emily opened the door, and she put her fingers to her lips as an indication to be very quiet, as the household dwellers were still all asleep. I acknowledged that I understood, and we proceeded into the home. I had just closed the door, turned around to continue into the dwelling, and Emily grabbed me into an embrace, our lips connected and the passion consumed us. We headed upstairs, to the bedroom, and fell into the bed, two bodies as one. We made love, but a more restricted love, ever so aware that too much noise would awaken the household and our secret would be out. We held each other after making love; but this too quickly ceased as the sounds from the bathroom stopped. Emily said *"You better leave quickly, before the person comes out of the bathroom"*.

In a flash, I grabbed my clothes, headed down the stairway and didn't stop to get dressed till I was on the outside. Thank God it was early morning and there were no people on the street; everything was still quiet, except for the chirping of the birds, welcoming the start of another new day.

I chuckled to myself as I headed home. The birds were chirping to start the day and I had started the day making love, although restrictive, nonetheless very enjoyable. My mother was just starting to stir as I headed upstairs to my room, to change my clothes, have my shave and shower, and get ready to head to work. When I came downstairs and into our kitchen, my mother said *"It seems that you got your morning walk in today. How's that for starting the day?"* I just smiled at her, and thought to myself, Mom if you only knew how great a start to my day that I just had, you would probably faint right there on the kitchen floor.

For the rest of the week, the routine was the same. Emily would take her husband Ken to work; come home to my welcoming arms, and we would head into their home and bedroom for a love-making session. I had the best of both worlds . . . my freedom to do as I pleased with both my time and money. On the other hand, I had a woman to make love to every day, with no commitments.

My bubble was soon to burst, as Emily started to develop feelings, and I wanted more time with her and the pleasure of making love. Emily soon asked me just what I wanted from her . . . just love-making, or was I willing to go the whole nine yards and make a commitment. Fortunately I had a logical reason why I could not make a commitment to her. *"You're married" I said.* Emily said that she wanted to leave Ken to begin a new life with me and to be happy again.

I am not too proud of this part of my life, as I told a white lie and said *"Emily I do want you in my life; you are my life now".* Emily was filled with emotion and began weeping profusely, I held her and told again another lie that everything would be okay and we would be happy together. There was no love-making this day, because all the time had been spent talking . . . not the usual good start of the day for me.

I was heading home. Again my mother was stirring, to start the day as I headed towards my bedroom to change, then shave and shower and go down for breakfast.

My mother said *"Son, you do not look happy this morning. In fact you look very serious, is something wrong?"* I would have loved to confide in her about my troubles; but would or could she understand? Would she in fact be upset with my behaviour? Would my parents want me out of their house for the way I was behaving?

Fortunately or not, time was ticking, and I had to get to work, so a simple, light-hearted reply of *"No Mom. Whatever gave you that idea? Everything is all right."* The weekend was now here. That meant that dear old Ken would be at home, and there would be no chance for a get together with Emily. I really had no plans for the weekend. So Saturday afternoon I decided to wash and wax my car out in front of my home.

Emily must have spotted me out there, and had made up a story to Ken that she needed to go to the variety store for something or other. As Emily walked towards me, she was talking in a low voice, and said that Ken would be leaving to go to another union meeting shortly, and that she had asked Nell if she would look after the kids for a couple of hours. She wanted to visit her girlfriend and go for a coffee without the children.

Emily said *"I'll meet you at 2:30 p. m. at the rear of the old abandoned fire hall building"*, and with that she was off to the store. Emily returned from the store and said out of the corner of her mouth, *"You are going to be there aren't you"*? I replied *"Indeed I will; looking forward to it"*. Fortunately, I had not yet started to wax my car and I quickly dried off the rear of the car and I was done. I thought that was good timing; but the waxing would have to wait.

As I entered the house my mother said *"Are you done already?"* and I told her that I thought I would hold off on the waxing of the car, since it did not look that bad. Next weekend was going to be a long weekend and I would have more time to spend, making the car sparkle. I told my Mom that *"I was going to cruise the main street to show off my shining car and see who in fact might be around to get together with this weekend."*

I made my way to the old abandoned fire hall building and parked at the rear to wait for Emily. She was about a half hour late; but that could not be helped, since Ken was a little later in leaving before she could get away.

Emily said she was sorry but knew that hopefully I would understand and be patient. She gave me a long, hard, passionate kiss, and said she couldn't wait to be with me again, to be held in my arms and that it was hell at home. I liked everything she said up to the point of "hell at home"! I could see Emily wanted to talk, to make our plans for our future. I was going to have to be creative here, to find the perfect way to both make her happy and to get what I wanted from our little get-together.

I was skilful, allowing her to vent her anger at her life with Ken . . . how unhappy she was, how her kids were aware that problems existed on the home front, that even her mother-in-law suspected that something was going on, that she could not stand it anymore. I held her and gave her small kisses on the cheek, and told her that we would eventually work things out. She drew herself away from me at this point, and said *"What does that mean . . . eventually"*?

With some quick thinking on my part, I told her that I needed a little time to save a little more money, for a down payment on a house before we could be together and start a life. This had done its trick. She was confident that our relationship was heading in a positive direction. Once again she became affectionate . . . kissing, touching, caressing one another's bodies, filling the desire to be as one, and then being one. The love-making was more passionate, more feeling, more fulfilling, as though this would be the last time we would ever make love. All too soon, the time approached for Emily to leave, and I was once again left alone.

I must have had some insight into the fact that it would be awhile before we did indeed make love again. Ken seemed to be staying home more, working from the house as I later found out, and preparing for a major union conference in Toronto. Emily had been out in her front yard playing with the children, and I made a point of saying hello to her, and then proceeded to sit down on my front porch. The children's ball had rolled over towards my home, and Emily quickly went after it to have an opportunity to speak with me and told me to be patient and she would be in touch with me soon.

Time seemed to move slowly on, for what seemed an eternity, and no other opportunity to speak with Emily availed itself. In fact it was a full week and a half before I even saw her again, and then she was with dear old Ken getting into their car and taking him off to work, or so I hoped.

I had been maintaining my usual morning routine, thank God. Nothing seemed out of sorts even to my parents, if they had indeed stirred. I quickly got dressed and hurried down to the gas station to get my car, before Emily returned home. The timing couldn't have been better time because we both arrived in front of our homes at the same moment.

Emily got out of her car first, and darted towards my car. Being a gentleman, I threw open the passenger door for her. Emily explained that she did not have time to stay, as her husband had forgotten his briefcase. She had come home to get it, and return to his work immediately. She could see the sadness in my eyes that we would not have some time together, and leaned over and kissed me passionately. I was starting to get excited, and she quickly pulled herself away from me.

Emily said *"Please Paul, stop. I do have to get going; but I miss you and need to kiss and talk with you. It has been so long"*. With that she opened the car door, leaned her head in again for another kiss, and said *"Ken is going out of town again for the whole weekend; so we will be together soon"*.

It was going to be another long week, but at least I had something to look forward to on the weekend. Finally Friday arrived, and I knew that Emily and I would have our morning get-together, and I waited for the sound of their Volkswagen to roar down the street. I quickly headed out of the house to go down and get my car at the station. I was totally surprised when a car pulled up in front of their home and I saw her mother-in-law getting out of the car. Where was Emily? How were we going to make our weekend plans?

I spoke to Nell and said *"Good morning"*. She said that she was not impressed with having to be up so early to take her son to work . . . *"Damn flu bug anyway"*. My first impression was that she did not seem like a morning person, and definitely not very friendly at this hour. Nell was soon on her way into the house; but she had given me all the information that I needed, and I was grateful. I did not know how to pose the questions that I really wanted to ask her.

I did catch a glimpse of Emily at her upstairs bedroom window, and she waved at me and threw me a kiss, and was gone. I wondered to myself whether I would see her on the weekend, and could only hope that it was the 24 hour flu bug and nothing more serious. It was not until Sunday morning that I heard the car engine roar down the street, and for some reason I looked out the window and saw Emily, walking past my house. My family had gone to Church; so I quickly ran to the doorway and shouted to her. Emily turned quickly at the sound of my voice, and I told her that I was alone. My parents had gone to Church. Emily replied that her mother-in-law and the kids had gone to Church as well.

She almost ran to my doorway, and instantly we were in each other's arms. We kissed and hugged each other as we went upstairs to my bedroom. It was almost as if destiny had worked a plan for everyone else to disappear so that we could be alone. In a heartbeat, we were scrambling to get out of our clothes and into bed. The long awaited pleasure had returned, and the passionate love-making was setting off explosions in my head. The pleasure was indescribable, and finally we were satisfied, and lay there in a sweaty pile of jumbled sheets.

I looked at the clock, and Emily said *"Got an appointment buddy?"* then she laughed. I told her that I did not want either of us getting caught . . . me with her in my bed, or her going out of my house and her mother-in-law pulling up in front of their home. Emily said

"Someday soon your parents and my family will know of our love and our wanting to be together".

I felt the pressure mounting inside my head with this statement, and I quickly searched my mind for an adequate response. The only thought that came out of my mouth was to say *"Yes, my darling; our love will be known by our families. But look at the time".* It started out emotionally, but then reality set in. It was close to noon, and my parents would be home shortly from Church. Saved by the clock! She seemed pleased by my response. We had enjoyed great sex; but this serious side to Emily was starting to bother me.

I did not want a ready-made family, plus have an older woman for a wife. I was young, and was in this affair only for the great sex . . . not a permanent arrangement. Boy, I was in it up to my neck in the permeable pile of dung. I knew I would have to think of a way to end this. But is there ever a good way to end a relationship? However, I thought this was not really a relationship with this woman. We were not dating as a couple but we were enjoying sex, great sex indeed . . . but just from my perspective. How had things gotten to the point that Emily thought we were to be together for the rest of our lives?

The light finally dawned. What else she would think from the comments I had been saying? But I had to say the things she wanted to hear, in order for the sex to continue and my pleasure level to be maintained.

I guess I had been selfish in my desires, but what the heck; she was the one that started this whole affair, way back when I was painting the porch at the rear of my family home. She was the instigator; she got the paint on her hands, supposedly by mistake; she planned this and knew how to play me, and sex was to be the tool.

In my mind at least, I shifted the blame from myself, and put it totally on her. In all fairness, it was probably a 50/50 deal; but in the end, she would still come out ahead in this arrangement. She would get out of the unhappiness in her present home life, and move herself and her kids in with me and my "new home".

For Emily, family life seemed to be ever more demanding of her time. We did not see each other much. As it turned out, her husband Ken was now the head union representative at work. His hours of work turned into a different timetable than mine; so that morning get-togethers were lost. If Emily was going to the store, she now had her children with her, or was in the company of her mother-in-law on a more regular basis.

It appeared to me that something had definitely changed; but I was not upset about it. It seemed to me that I would not have to come up with any excuses for us to stop seeing each other. That had already been done for me. Occasionally, Emily and I would see each other, on the way to our cars, on the way to or coming from the variety store, out in public places, and so on. But every time she had company tagging along, so we never had any "real time" to chat, than just a "hello" or to talk about the weather, and a impersonal "have a good day" as we passed like two ships at sea heading in opposite directions.

I could see the pain in Emily's eyes, and felt her unhappiness; but all this was totally outside my control. That was exactly how I wanted it to be. It's not because I was not without feelings for this lady; but more importantly, our relationship had to end. I did not want to be harnessed to this woman and her kids for the rest of my life.

I knew from her past record that if I had become connected to her on a permanent basis, that if or when, she became unhappy again, she would seek out another male companion. And so the cycle would continue. I would then be on the receiving end of heartache, just like good old Ken. I never liked the man, or what Emily told me about his temper and meanness to her; but I was just getting her side of the story. Nevertheless, something in my gut took an instant dislike to this man; but I could not for the life of me, tell what it was.

One day as fate would have it, Emily was heading to the variety store alone and I was sitting alone on the front porch. She stopped, gave me a smile, and waited for a friendly greeting. She asked if I would walk with her down to the variety store, in order that we might re-connect. Perhaps we might even make some plans to see one other again.

I stood up and proceeded to the stairway, and was soon standing beside her. Emily commented that it seemed strange that we were not kissing and hugging, because we would usually have been doing so. I told her that I understood; but that there were people around, and we would only complicate the situation . . . it was not because I did not want to.

This brought a brief half smile from her, but she did not seem convinced with my explanation. We walked in silence for awhile. She wanted to hold my hand, and I told her that we could not do so in public. I guess women's intuition quickly took over, and she said *"You do not want me anymore do you"*? A huge lump was instantly in my throat; I wanted to say the right thing, do the right thing, and make her heart lighter and put laughter in her spirit.

I could not bring myself to do this; I was a heel. It seemed I was only concerned for my own happiness . . . maybe a selfish bastard; but a least an honest one. I told Emily that it was for the best; that possibly she and Ken could re-build their relationship; that life could be rich and full with happiness just like before, if she gave it a chance.

At this point she starting crying, a painful sound to even the hardest of heartless heels, and she turned and started to run for home. I grabbed her arm and said *"We need to talk, to iron things out"*. Would she meet up with me?

She said that we had better "buster". So we were to meet that night at 8:00 p.m. at the public school right around the corner. It was the hardest thing for me to walk around the corner. My legs and my heart were heavy. I wanted to do the right thing, but for the wrong reasons. Or was it the wrong thing for the right reasons? I watched Emily approach the schoolyard, and we walked in silence around to the fire chute area. Fond memories of playful times within the wall structure danced in my head. Soon we were behind the fire chute.

I was surprised when Emily grabbed me and kissed me passionately and naturally, I responded. She told me that she was sorry for her actions; but she had missed me and making love with me had made her feel alive. She said that life was still hell on the home front and that she wanted a divorce from Ken and had told him so. She took my "not being happy" mood, when we had started walking to the variety store the wrong way. She had hoped and also realized that she was punishing me, before I had a chance to defend myself.

I told Emily that I was not sure about being a step-father to her kids. I had feelings for her, but not for her kids. This would be the wrong way to go into a relationship and I didn't think that time would change my feelings. At this point Emily started to cry, and even I felt the tears rolling down my own cheeks. Emily asked, *"Is it because we hadn't seen each other for awhile?"* She told me that Ken had suspected something was not right with Emily and her positive change in attitude. He felt she was cheating on him: so Emily lied and said there was nothing going on. Ken insisted that Emily be with the kids or his mother whenever she was out and about.

Emily had to go along with this demand just to keep harmony on the home front and that is why they did not see each other. Emily went on about her love and her wants and wishing a good life with me and how she would make me happy. But she could see that her wish for a life with me was hopeless.

I knew at that moment that we both had to walk away, before she cried more. I weakened and let my guard down; but I made her happy and me unhappy. It was the hardest first step I had ever taken; then I took another and another. I could still hear her crying as I was nearing home. I felt ashamed of myself, my lust, my inability to not hurt another person. I thought that I did not deserve happiness when I was such a rotten person . . . not capable to love or be loved.

That had been my decision and I was going to have to live with it for the rest of my life. It might have worked out had I been man enough to give it a chance.

I was a young lad, not yet a man, and so did not have the willpower or the backbone to make a proper, logical decision, one that may have brought me happiness for the rest of my life; but I will never know. How sad is that?

It was not long after Emily and I had our last meeting that a sign showing the property was for sale was evident on the front lawn. It didn't take long and the house was sold. A moving truck soon followed, and new resident owners were in place.

In later months I had heard Ken had had a car accident and had died. I had also heard that Emily had quickly found a new husband to replace Ken and that she and her kids were now out living in the country some 40 minutes from where she used to live.

As God, is my witness, I did pray that Emily's new husband would treat her well and make a happy life for her and the kids. I thought that, but for the Grace of God, it could have been me. Very possibly I would have known happiness and contentment; but I had not made that decision and would have to struggle with not knowing for the rest of my life.

Once again, I returned to an empty life . . . a life of a regular routine of work, home and loneliness. I had still been dating Erin all through my time with Emily. What I *should* be stating is that I was always waiting for the phone to ring to give me an "audience" with Erin and her entourage. As I said, I was in a nineteen year relationship "of sorts" and this was probably my punishment for the way I had let Emily down, or so I believed.

When Erin and I connected for a date, she commented that I looked different, a regular "sad sack". How nice a comment is that from a supposed girlfriend? In reality, Erin had hit the nail on the head. I had let Emily slip away along with the love and happiness, to return to being unloved and sad. I told Erin that I had missed her and spending time together, and she actually kissed me. I thought, don't hurt yourself honey; but did manage to muster a smile of appreciation. She told me that it was entirely my fault that she did not want to spend a lot of time with me. I asked her what she meant by this comment and she explained that I was too serious.

I wanted to get married and start a family. I thought to myself, was this not a normal approach to a committed relationship? Where was my head? Was I a total idiot to think that this shouldn't be a normal path for two people who were supposed to be in love? Erin explained to me, that I must be as thick as a brick, not to realize that she wanted time to party and have fun. Just because I was ready, didn't mean that she was.

I guess in all fairness, Erin had graduated as a registered nurse not that terribly long ago, and her logic did make sense. Perhaps a few months or maybe a year of freedom, she might come around to my way of thinking. At least I hoped so.

Time marched on, and so did the infrequent dates with Erin, when she could fit me into her schedule. I went along for the ride, because I was an ass and had no backbone and let Erin take full charge of when we would see each other and the time allowed for our getting together.

My parents, friends, and co-workers all told me that I was stupid to allow a lady to have this much control over me. Why did I not just break off the relationship? I really did not have a single good reason not to drop Erin, except in my heart. I hoped that everything would eventually work out. I was hoping to show those people that my endurance did indeed come to a successful conclusion. Probably the only reason that I did really did have, was that if I let Erin go, I would definitely have nobody in my life.

I had convinced myself that I could not find another girl. I was a loser! My self-esteem was at an all time low. How would I ever get another date, if I said goodbye to Erin? The dating, although sporadic, still was a life line of hope to me. So time marched on, and on. Erin had re-united herself with past friends and school mates. So, it was a major surprise to me when she stated that she and an old classmate were moving in together.

They had signed a lease on a two-storey townhouse and would be moving in that upcoming weekend. Erin was telling me all this in a phone call, which was totally out of the ordinary. Normally, Erin would only call on Fridays, if she remembered to see if I wanted to hang out with the group. This was Thursday night and Erin's voice sounded so happy. I hadn't heard her like this in a long time; but there was a reason for this call. Would I give her some help moving furniture on the weekend?

Finally she needed me. Like an idiot, I agreed to help her out and hence the nice sweet voice. She was looking forward to seeing me soon!

Like a dog, I had been summoned to London for the weekend, and like a good dog, I wagged my tail and said I would be there to help. As I look back at myself during this period, I am ashamed once again.

The weekend came and I was heading to London to be the pack mule for Erin to direct the moving procedure. One good point in Erin's favour was that she or her new roommate had arranged for plenty of help to make the move an easy one. With all the people participating, it did not take too long and the move was done.

Some of the people that helped with the move, stayed a brief time after the job had been completed. The beer flowed freely, and the entire atmosphere was party-like. So many others settled in for the duration of the day. For some reason, Erin was very friendly towards me . . . exceptionally friendly, more than I was used to. I soon discovered why.

All the boxes needed to be emptied, and carried to different parts of the house, and then the boxes needed to be broken down. Furniture needed to be re-arranged, appliances needed cleaning out, food needed to be put in cupboards, and so on. Most of the helpers were busy partying. The only thing that was missing as Erin barked out her orders was a whip in her hands. Then the picture of a "Ring Master" would have made it perfect.

When the house was finally put in good shape, or at least to Erin's liking, the few people who actually were in the home organizing it, went outside to join the party animals. It was at this point that Erin actually introduced me to the lady that was going to live with her. I had seen her inside helping; but never was told that she was the one going to live there. I was probably the last person of the group to know this. Why would anyone not bother to point this out to me?

I was told her name was Rebecca and had been Erin's best friend for years. She was a school teacher, and was going to teach at a school nearby. So it came about that Erin and she talked, and the rest is history. I really felt my feelings had been hurt. I was the last to know who was moving in.

This just re-enforced the fact that I was not very special to Erin. I was useful but not special; I was just an object to control. I told Erin that I was tired and probably should head for home. She told me to hang around because food had been ordered. I was hoping for a little praise from Erin, for all my help; but this was not forthcoming. Instead she said *"Have a drink."* I do not know for the life of me, why I expected positive reinforcement from Erin, when that was never in her character. In reality she was a very cold fish!! I was really getting to see the entire picture of Erin; something that I either hid from myself or would not allow myself to notice.

The drinking continued; the food soon arrived; and the good times rolled. It was getting late in the evening and a lot of the men were drunk. Their wives, being sober, were trying to get them into the cars. I could not believe the quantity of beverages that had been consumed. I had only drunk in moderation. Erin, being the good hostess had passed out probably a good hour, before the end of the evening. I couldn't stand the mess both inside and outside. This is a flaw in my characters – neatness. So I busied myself with the clean up. I had done a pretty good job of picking up all the empty beer bottles and food on the outside and headed inside, to start working there.

I was the only person left to do the work because, either everyone had gone to bed, or had left for home. I busied myself again, picking up empties and leftover food items scattered everywhere. I could not believe that people acted pretty much like wild animals, with no consideration for someone else's home. I was not impressed!

I had pretty well finished the job and was about to go out the doorway heading home, when Rebecca came down the staircase. As she headed in my direction she bounced off the wall and stair railing on her descent. She slurred out *"What shah doing?"* I told her I couldn't stand the mess the house was in, so I had just finished cleaning the mess up.

Rebecca said *"I think you need to be rewarded; come and have another drink with me"*. I helped her over to the couch, and asked her if she really wanted another drink. At this point she pulled me towards her and started to kiss me. Being a gentleman, I responded and I thought "what the heck". A little reward was indeed in order. Our kissing became more intense. Both of us allowed our hands to wander over each other's bodies. Soon her hands were on my trousers pulling at my zipper. All Rebecca had on was a see-through nightie and I was already enjoying looking at her body, and soon she had me naked.

We had just finished making love on the couch when who should come stumbling down the staircase, but Erin. It was an amazing transition from drunk/sleepy to sober/totally awake. She screamed *"What the hell is going on?"* as she headed in our direction. Erin screamed at Rebecca *"Get to bed and you, Paul get the hell out"*!

As I drove home, I thought, well if it is over with Erin, at least it ended with a bang, but not from Erin. But dear Rebecca had come through for me. I was not the least bit hurt emotionally, since Erin and I were just going through the "act of being a couple", and maybe it was time to end this display. It now had been many years of non-emotional, no commitment to one another. I had had enough, and was ready to move on.

Erin called the next morning and said *"I am coming down to talk to you mister; so you had better have some good reasons for your actions last night"*. I could not believe my ears, as I hung up the phone. What the hell is she up to now? I started to seek answers in my mind as to why she was possibly coming down. I thought it was all over last night; but surely she had more to say. Just what was her motive? I had not long to wait. It seemed an instant . . . certainly no more than 30 minutes . . . a knock was heard and the door was opening at the same time.

Erin stormed in, even before I could get off the couch. She was screaming all kinds of nasty comments; her arms waving hysterically with both fists clenched. I actually thought that she would/wanted to hit me, as though that would clear the air. I said nothing in response to her comments; but rather took the non-responsive mode to her aggressive behaviour. This seemed to be working, a sort of reverse physiology. Let her burn herself out. Then maybe I could get a word in edgeways.

Finally, Erin was becoming a little more rational. There was a calmer expression on her face, to the point where I thought I might now begin to talk to her. I explained that I had merely been doing the cleanup of the mess, when Rebecca surprised me with her presence in the living room.

Because she was plainly drunk and I had merely tried to help her to the couch. That is when she took advantage of me. Plainly I had reverted back to being a mouse, having no backbone, passing all the responsibility onto Rebecca. In my mind I could not believe what I was saying.

But it was indeed coming out of my mouth. Why, was I being so gutless? What hold did Erin have on me? Why was I so scared? Why did I even want to hang onto this so-called relationship? Why was I so afraid of being alone without anyone?

Erin stated that Rebecca had really no recollection of what had happened last night and said she was sorry to Erin. Erin said because of that, she was going to give me another chance. I guess my non-responsive tactics had worked. In actual fact, it was the only method that might have saved my ass . . . at least on this occasion. I made coffee and we chatted like an old married couple, as though the whole ordeal was only a dream in Erin's mind.

Erin soon left after the coffee was finished; but to my surprise actually gave me a kiss and said she would talk with me through the week. You could have knocked me down with a feather. What the hell had just happened? Was I in a dream?

But to my surprise, Wednesday of that week Erin did call and said we should go to a show this coming weekend. I could not believe my ears. We should go to a movie, just the two of us? I waited the rest of the week, in suspense. What was her motive? What was she really planning?

I called her Friday night, and indeed she said it was a go for Saturday. I should come early, and we could browse through the paper to select the show we were going to see. Like a little puppy, I complied with her wishes, and arrived just after the lunch hour. We chatted and flipped through the paper, as though we were a regular, dating couple.

This did not feel right to me. This is what I wanted, but somehow, something ate at my gut. In my defence, I waited for the boom to be lowered on my head. I cannot say that I enjoyed my stay with Erin; or that I really had any knowledge of the show. In fact, I had no memory of that whole Saturday.

What was Erin up to? This was just like when we first started to date. We were strictly a couple and doing what couples were supposed to do; or what I "perceived" what couples should be doing. I was even asked to her mother's for Sunday lunch the next day. Boy whatever she was up to, she had me totally confused.

If indeed she had a plan of action, it was working perfectly on me. I did not know what to expect next. As soon as I entered Erin's mother's home, I was greeted by the family. Guess what. Rebecca was there for lunch also. Lunch was their big meal of the day; so it was a full course meal, including home-made desserts. Erin's father got out his home-made wine, and her parents still treated me like the future son-in-law. But, I was still waiting for the bomb to drop. It did not seem to be forthcoming.

It was like the past weekends, when Erin and I first started dating. Everybody was happy to see one another, and a future seemed possible. Even Erin and Rebecca seemed to be on good speaking terms; all seemed back to normal.

Normal indeed . . . Erin was going on a holiday with Rebecca. They were going to Cuba for a two week vacation. Was this Erin's plan to treat me nice, to keep me hanging around? She had done her "nice" stint, and now could go back to her normal ways, both with me and her life.

This vacation was a total surprise to me, and I said to Erin, *"What about me?"* Why was there no discussion about her plans? Did she not think that I should be aware of what she was planning? Was I not a person of worth? She tried to console me by saying that this would likely be her last holiday with Rebecca and that she was thinking more positively about us.

Guess it's like the circus saying "a sucker is born every minute". It sure fit me perfectly; I went for it hook, line, and sinker. Boy was I gullible. I really thought she meant that we were going to start a real relationship, leading to marriage and my goal in life to have a wife and children would finally be achieved.

The vacation time was quickly approaching, and my heart was sad to know that I would be totally alone again. Added to that, I wasn't even asked to the airport for her departure. It was as though she had disappeared from the face of the earth. The two week period seemed an eternity; but as in all things, time finally arrived for her to return home. I waited and waited for the phone to ring, announcing that she had arrived home, safe and sound.

The phone never rang, and I was at my wit's ends, as I tried to reach her at her home phone number. It was not till late in the evening of the next day that she did finally call. I told her that I had tried to reach her, calling several times.

I even left messages on her phone machine. Erin said *"Sorry, I forgot to call you when I got home; but Rebecca and I went to my sister's, and time just got away from us. When I eventually got home, it was too late to call; so here I am now, contacting you"*. I said, *"Well, nice of you to call. I hope you two had a good time"*. Erin just said *"You sound mad; so I will talk with you later"*.

I don't think that I was as mad, as I was deeply hurt, to know that I could be dismissed so casually. Guess it was really not too important a call for her to make. It was as if she had been successful again, in putting me in my place. The bomb had finally dropped and I knew that once again I was on the back burner in Erin's life.

Erin was busy with her work, her friends and her family commitments. Consequently, I did not see much of her for nearly a week and a half. Finally she must have realized that she had not spoken to me in awhile. So I was privileged to receive a call from her. I tried my best be happy to hear from her. But she must have still sensed in the tone of voice that I was not. Therefore, the call was short and sweet. She said *"Sorry, I have plans for this weekend as well. But hopefully we will get together the following weekend"*.

Like a fool, I said *"I hope you have a good weekend"*. *I'll look forward to getting together the next weekend."* I could not believe myself that I still put up with such treatment. Even my parents were complaining that she was treating me badly and I should drop her. I tried to defend Erin saying *"She needs to have some time to be with her friends"*. My parents replied, *"Yes some time with her friends; but what about time with you?"*

I knew my parents were right; but I was afraid to let go of the only existing relationship I seemed to have. In reality, I had a "non-relationship"; but I could just not see it. I had more lonely weekends and more non-existent phone calls in my future. I just went along with whatever Erin wanted, and like an animal she patted me on the head. Time weighed heavily on my heart, on my mind and on my very existence.

It was about this time, that a new lady entered my life. She was our new receptionist at work and she caught my attention, both when I heard her voice over the PA system and in real life when we finally met.

Her name was Amy, recently divorced with two kids, and was strictly here on a trial basis. I thought this story is just like Emily's. Amy wanted a divorce; she had two kids and was looking to go into another relationship and a possible career.

I didn't want that kind of relationship again, but I was not sure that Amy would want to date me either. I was possibly putting the horse before the cart. Hell I just met her, and I was already planning our first date.

As time when on, and a closer work relationship started, soon it was time to ask her out for a coffee after work to see if she would be interested. I was pleased to learn that indeed she would like to do that; but it would be hard to arrange, as her kids were in school and she needed to be at home on their return. I then suggested she arrange for a baby sitter, and that we have a dinner date. I was pleased that Amy thought that this would work better for all concerned, and the plan was put in motion.

Reality check. What about Erin, her friends, somebody seeing me out with Amy? I thought it was worth the gamble; I really did not have that much to lose. I laid out a clever plan, to have a late dinner, at some expensive restaurant, and the likelihood that I would run into somebody, would be remote.

Saturday night arrived, and I went to pick up Amy for our date. I was surprised to find out that she lived in a subsidized townhouse complex, where there seemed to be a lot of unmarried women and lots and lots of kids. This should have been my first clue, that I was entering the dragon's den, and may come to regret my actions. I thought that I could handle this. After all this may only be a one night affair.

Amy introduced me to her two children, a girl Kelly who was 14 years old, and the boy Chris who was 10 years old. They seemed like nice kids, but I was not really interested in them as much as in their mother. The red lights and bells should have been sounding off alarms; but I was totally unaware of the road I was now travelling. I had not been out with Erin for quite awhile. Hell I had not even spoken to her lately; so I deserved a good night out. I had taken Amy some yellow roses. I guess I was looking for brownie points and I took a bottle of nice wine . . . hopefully for later, if the night went well.

We both enjoyed the quiet atmosphere, soothing music and the dinner. Great conversation made it a totally enjoyable evening. I had forgotten what it was like to be out on a date, and had really gotten caught up in the moment. I had forgotten that it too was a first date for Amy in some time; so she was very impressed with the choice of the restaurant and the attention she was now receiving.

When I arrived back at Amy's, I was hopeful for a kiss, but really wanting to be invited in to drink some wine. I thought the evening was too early to draw to a close. I was very pleased as I walked her to her doorway, gave her a kiss, and was about to leave and she asked if I would like to come in for a drink of wine. How great is that! It was as though she had read my mind. However, in reality I was just putty in her capable hands, and getting led down the path already set, that she had prepared.

We entered her home, and she said to make myself comfortable in the living room, while she got us some wine. I smiled, and walked towards the area she had pointed for me to go to. We sat in a dimly lit room, wine in our hands; close to one another, and then she leaned over and kissed me. It was a passionate kiss, the kind of which I had not enjoyed in a very long time.

We became more entwined in each other's arms and the passion was filling the air. Amy excused herself, only to return in a few minutes, wearing only a see through purple nightie, the light of the room displaying the curvy body within. A moment of making love was about to begin. It had been a long time for the both of us, enjoying the pleasures that come with union of two bodies. The lights and rockets went off for some time, till the pleasure cup was full.

The drive to my parent's home was a totally unknown drive to me, the date, the pleasures of making love, the feeling of wholeness once again returned. Now what was I going to do?

I decided to just go with the flow, and try dating the two of them at the same time . . . not too big a chore to handle. I knew that Erin was an on-again, off-again type of arrangement, so that shouldn't pose a problem. With Amy, I could dance around any situation that might show itself. It could be fun to at least try it on for size. Let the games begin!!

I had not planned to get into too a serious relationship with Amy. I thought that if I had known in advance about her pre-planned thoughts, then I could simply have walked away. Who am I kidding here?

I had just had the greatest sex from Amy and Erin hadn't even shown any affection to me in a long time. I was now been led by another part of my body, my "lust zone" and was not using any logical thinking at this point at all. I did not know that I had been trapped; but hindsight is a great thing, and trapped I was. I looked forward to seeing Amy at work and making plans to do things together on the weekend.

Life had become rich and full once again. Amy would made arrangements with her ex-husband to have the children some weekends. Her parents were always happy to have the grandchildren come to their home on the weekends that their father couldn't help out. It was if Amy and I were just two single people enjoying life together and finding ourselves within each other.

Here in, was the major fault in the relationship. There were kids to consider when Amy and I planned an outing and I did not include them in my calculations for any of our future outings. The shock zone that lay ahead would be a total reality check. It would be the beginning and ending of any relationship with Amy. But for the time being, this was not an issue for several months to come.

Amy and I planned a summer vacation that very first year of our relationship. I had rented a cottage in Perry Sound for a two week get-away. Her parents stepped up to the plate and announced that it would be no problem to have the kids for that time period, so everything was a go.

When we arrived at the cottage, Amy's attitude was not long in changing. The cottage was a little too rustic for her and I think in her mind, she had expected a resort-type get away . . . not one where she and I would be doing the meals, the clean-up, and some general housework. I started to see a different side to Amy, than I had seen before. Now there should have been some bells going off in my head. Once we settled in, a little "kiss ass" on my part and then taking her out for dinner, helped change her mood.

That evening, all was as it had been in the beginning. We built a fire in the mammoth fieldstone fireplace and opened a bottle of wine and the romantic mood was in full swing. Amy had again brought along a see-through nightie and her curvy body was illuminated by the glow of the fireplace. In an instant, our bodies were intertwined and the evening of pleasure extended into the early dawn. We actually had to go to bed to get rested up before we went outside in the sun, later in the morning.

We had a private sandy beach just out of the cabin doorway, and the lake was calm, cool, and inviting. We both rushed to the water's edge, although Amy stopped at this point, while I carried on into the water. Amy said *"It's too cold for me. I am just going to lay here on the beach and you can stay in if you wish"*. I found it a little too fresh for my liking too; but could not be a sissy. So, I prolonged it for as long as possible and was happy to be out and joining her in the warmth of the sun.

Once, Amy put her mind to it she became a little more happy with the accommodation. Since I did most of the barbequing for the meals, she thought it really wasn't that bad. The two weeks went by quickly, and soon we were on our way back home and to our regular schedules.

Erin had called and left a few messages on my personal answering machine. Thank God I had taken Amy home and consequently, she did not know about any of these calls.

Erin knew that I would be home on the Saturday and was having a party that night and expected me to be there. I called her and told her about how I needed to do some jobs and laundry before going back to work and that I would see her on Monday. She said *"That's good because I have things to do and need some time with my kids; so have a good weekend and I will talk to you later"*. I was worried about that comment "talk with you later", and hoped she didn't call till Sunday at the earliest . . . if at all.

Saturday evening was the usual greeting from Erin upon my arrival there. A quick kiss at the doorway she quickly asked if I had a nice vacation, all the time walking towards Rebecca, waiting in the kitchen. Rebecca smiled at me and said *"Welcome back. Have a good vacation?"* At least she appeared to have missed me, and I was to find out later that evening how much Rebecca really had missed me.

The usual people started to arrive for the party, and like the good man-servant, Erin put me to work . . . making her guests feel welcome and helping bring food and drink to them. The party atmosphere carried on till nearly 1:00 a.m. and as quickly as they had arrived they were gone. The mess was left behind, and so was Erin, having passed out nearly an hour before the end of the party. I was really tired, (probably was feeling the booze) and decided to stay the night, and help with the clean up next morning.

I had gone down to the third bedroom, and had stripped off my clothes, and was just climbing into the bed, when a knock was on the wall of my bedroom. I walked down to Rebecca's room, poked my head in, and asked if she wanted something. She threw back the bedding, exposing her nude body, and said *"Come here big boy"*. I could not resist. I am only human, and it had been awhile since my one night of making love with Rebecca, and Erin was definitely out of the picture.

I went to the first bedroom to make sure that Erin was still long gone in her drunken state; then quickly returned to Rebecca's room and slipped into the open bedding and her warm body. It was the highlight of the party and it was just a party of two. Rebecca was totally longing for love and we carried on into the wee hours of the morning. I had just gotten up and was heading into the bathroom when Erin's bedroom door opened and with a glassy stare said *"What you doing here"?* I said that I was also too drunk to drive home, and was now just getting up to put on the coffee and start the cleanup routine. Erin said *"Aren't you a good boy"* and she headed back to her bedroom to start getting dressed as well. I looked into Rebecca's bedroom and she said softly *"Yes, you were a really good boy"*. Then she just smiled and rolled over.

After breakfast and the cleanup routine was complete, I said I had better get home and do some work in preparation for Monday and the week that lay ahead. Both girls waved a friendly good-bye and I was off to my parent's home, along with a well-deserved restful day of leisure. My thoughts of leisure quickly came to a halt when I got home. Amy had called and left a message inviting me to her home for a Sunday dinner. She said *"It's the least I can do to show my appreciation for the holiday you took me on"*. I called Amy and told her I would be very happy to come and thanked her for the invite.

She asked if I got all my jobs and laundry caught up, and I lied and said *"Yes Amy, I did a lot of work on Saturday and was happy to have the time to get it done"*. I told a little lie; but in my defence, I had done the laundry, but did little else.

It was a totally different experience, sitting at Amy's kitchen table with her two kids staring at me. Amy was busy at the stove, getting the meal ready for the table. It was like a normal family gathering (or at least much like I had experienced as a child at my parent's table); but it felt neither comfortable nor real. I was "on display" for Amy's kids to judge and for her to see how I would handle the situation. I must have passed with flying colors, because Amy smiled happily at me, and then busied herself cleaning up.

I asked if I could help out, but she said *"You are still a guest at my table; but once we are living together, I will expect that to happen"*. You could have knocked me down with a feather with that last comment.

Now the plot started to thicken as I had earlier mentioned. She had been planning her strategy all along, and was slowly starting to ease into phase one. I told her jokingly that we will have to talk about that when that time came around; but her stare could have stopped an eight-day clock!

She told her kids to go outside and play for awhile. It would soon be time to come in to get ready for bed. Amy asked me if I would like a coffee or glass of wine, and she would bring it to me in the living room. I knew that the shit would soon be hitting the fan, just from that piercing stare she had delivered; but I complied with her wishes.

Yes, my gut instinct was correct. Indeed she wanted to know where our relationship was heading and what, when and how it was going to be put in place. I guess you could say I was "read the riot act" and had to do a lot of soft peddling to keep things from heading south. I really enjoyed sex with Amy, the best in a long time. But my thoughts were also of Rebecca; she was quite satisfying and it was looking as if it would continue. I think also I was wondering if Erin would soon be coming around.

It was a major challenge, much like the fox and hounds. Amy was crying at this point and I had not spoken too many words in my defence. She thought that I was being indifferent to her wishes and desires. I soon regained my composure and told her that I was just thinking about her and her kids and our life together and the whole nine yards.

In reality, I was really thinking that I wanted out of here and did NOT want to be forced into making decisions on the spot. I told Amy a little lie and said I wanted her but that I needed time to adjust to her kids and having them around. This seemed to do the trick for the time being and she kissed me again passionately. She said *"I hope you are not in a hurry to leave"*. Well, now I was in a real pickle. Should I run, or should I stay and have great sex?

What part of my body do you think made that decision for me? I settled in the easy chair with my glass of wine and was just enjoying the quiet moment and unwinding from the stress of the conversation moments before. Soon, I heard Amy calling in her kids to come in and get ready for bed. It sounded like a herd of elephants going up the staircase, as all three were running up the stairs, to get cleaned up and into bed. I thought to myself, God I hope this is not a nightly ordeal; this would drive me crazy. It really broke the calm and quiet of the moment. Soon I heard softer sounds coming from the second floor. At last peace and quiet had been restored. All was well in my world again, and now the good times could follow. Amy made an appearance again in a soft green see-through nightie. As she turned off the lights, again the curvy body was silhouetted against the shadowed background of a single, dimly lit lamp.

Amy crossed over the room to where I was sitting and positioned herself atop my both legs. Amy said is a very sexy voice*," See anything you like big boy?"* I could not contain myself and quickly had my hands on her breasts and rubbing her thighs. As we started kissing, Amy's hands were on my pants, undoing them and pulling them down. Moments later as we were making love, the fantastic rush that was going through my head and every other part of my body, was broken with these words *"Mommy I do not feel well"*. Amy quickly jump off my body, and told her son she was coming, (so was I if anybody cared). She was off upstairs, only to return a few minutes later.

She said, *"I'm sorry, but Chris has a bit of a fever, and would you mind going home now? I'll see you tomorrow"*.

Boy, did this lady know the condition she left me in? I said *"I can wait a few minutes till you return"*. I wanted to finish what we had started, and so did my body. Amy told me *"I really have to look after Chris and it may be a bit of time, so it is best for you to go"*.

I said to myself, that is what I want to do; to go as well. I headed out the doorway with a quick kiss goodbye from Amy, and soon was heading to my parent's home. I felt totally unsatisfied and rejected. It may be a little selfish on my part; but hey I was in this only for sex. I was not really looking for a family relationship. I thought, what the hell. Had I wanted to go down this road? HELL NO! However, this is the road I was seemingly going on and I had better get a grip on myself. I had better start thinking with my mind rather than my penis!!

Monday morning and Amy was at my desk. Amy apologized for the quick ending from the night before, and told me that Chris was feeling better, and had gone to school. I thought to myself, who really cares, I just wished he had not ruined my night of pleasure. I forced a smile of happiness and said *"I'm glad he is better"* and this seemed to make Amy happy once again.

Amy said *"See you later at coffee break"* and she was off to her work station. The week seemed to drag on and Amy seemed on a busy schedule with her kids and had no time to squeeze in a night of pleasure for me. I was thinking that this is what all the married men complained about. The kids take precedence over all other activities and by the weekend the wife is too tired to please her man. It was almost to the point where self-pity was starting to consume me.

My mother had decided to go back to school to get the nursing degree that she had always wanted, and had made the application for it. She stopped her dream of becoming a nurse when kids came along. I was proud that at her age, she still wanted to fulfill that dream. Dad and I were told that we would have to take on a lot more responsibilities, so that Mom would have time for her school work. Both Dad and I were happy to help out; but we had no idea how much work this lady did for us. It was a whole new learning experience for both of us.

On the up-side to this new lifestyle, my mother had a lot of single young ladies as classmates. She would often bring home one or two of them to either help her or she would help them with class assignments. My Mother was a good student, a good learner and she retained new information well. She also had a strong desire to be successful. Mom was a very dedicated student and her marks bore that out. Her fellow classmates were always happy when Mom could clear up a problem for them; hence she was often asked for assistance.

It was on one of these occasions, that I met one of her classmates, a lady by the name of Aerial. She had long brunette hair that hung past her shoulders, and a very well-put-together body. Best of all she had no current boyfriend. On one of her nights at our home, I made a comment that I was wondering whether she would like to go out for a drink with me. Aerial said that she and Mom would be finishing off a project on Wednesday night, and if it was not too late, we could go for that drink at that time.

After Aerial left, Mom said *"What about Erin and Amy? How are you going to work in three ladies at the same time?"* Then she said *"Aerial is a nice lady; do not do anything bad to hurt her feelings. Do you hear me"?* I told her *"I am just exploring other possibilities, and would see where this leads me, not getting too serious. At the moment; it is just a drink Mom."*

Wednesday finally rolled around, and true to form, Aerial and Mom were working on their project, and completion time was in sight. Aerial said at their first break time that they would probably finish within an hour and a half and did I wish to still go for that drink? I exclaimed that indeed I did, and to come to the recreation room to get me, when she was ready. The time seemed to drag on as it often tends to do, when you have planned to do something else. As I looked up from the TV, Aerial was standing there.

Aerial said *"I am ready to go if you are",* and with that I was on my feet and walking towards her. I explained that I appreciated her going out with me, and that I would not keep her late, since she must be tired. We said our goodbyes to my parents as we headed out the door, to my car, and off uptown for that drink. I made small talk with Aerial as I drove to the bar and soon we were enjoying that first drink together. Aerial asked if I had any plans for the upcoming weekend, because this would be her first free weekend without school work to be done. I was on the spot, so I smiled and said that nothing important was on my list, except spending time with her and getting to know her. Boy! My reply was as smooth as butter and to my surprise Aerial leaned over and gave me a kiss. We finished our drinks, and I said I had better get her home as the hour was getting late.

Mom was still up when I got home, and she asked me how it had gone with Aerial, and I said I was taking her out on the weekend. Mom just smiled kind of a mysterious smile and said it was late, that we both had better get to bed. I could not sleep because of all the thoughts racing through my head. First of all, where will I take Aerial? What would I tell Amy? If Erin was around, what would I say? I had been too smart for myself, and it looked like it was catching up to me. *"Boy"* I said. *"You had better put on your thinking cap and get yourself out of this predicament."*

When I saw Amy at work the next day, I asked her how she was and about her children. Amy smiled and said *"Great, thanks for asking. But I have a problem that I must talk to you about".* I wondered what possible problem could there be? She knew nothing of Aerial and of course I was feeling guilty. So, I regained my composure and waited to hear what was on her mind. Amy said that her parents wanted her and her kids to go to Canada's Wonderland for the weekend, so she would not be around. I wanted to jump for joy, say fantastic, but I realized that I had to play a different part. I said *"That's wonderful! You and your kids will have a great time".*

I even believed myself and was proud at how well I had sounded. Amy smiled, a wide smile, and said *"You are the greatest! I will call you when we get home". "Whew! One down and one to go."* So I decided to strike while the iron was hot. I went to my phone and called Erin at the hospital. I told her that a friend of mine I hadn't seen for sometime was in town this weekend, and I wanted to hook up with him. Erin said that worked out well, because she forgot to phone to let me know she and Rebecca had made plans to go away this weekend too.

I was not sure if I was hurt because of Erin's treatment of me, or whether I should be happy that I had my own plans for the weekend.

I called Aerial on Friday late afternoon and asked her preference for either that night, or Saturday. Aerial's response both surprised and delighted me. She said *"How about both nights?"* She giggled and then said *"We can get together literally if you like".* I could not believe my ears, she was propositioning me and it excited me. I was on cloud nine and didn't or couldn't come up with a response. When I regained my composure, I asked if she would like to go out for dinner tonight and she said *"How about you just come to my apartment and we will order in later."* I asked her what time she wanted me to come over, and she said *"What about now; are you busy"?*

How strange it felt with Aerial. She was in charge; but not like Erin. Aerial **wanted** to connect with me and not just give me excuses as to why we would not be getting together this particular weekend. I told Aerial I would pick up some wine and would be over shortly.

When I arrived at Aerial's apartment, she greeted me with a passionate kiss, and we headed for the couch. I don't know for sure, which of us was the horniest, but what did it matter? The important thing was that we were going to have sex immediately. We kissed and started to pull one another's clothes off . . . the passion for intimateness was strong, and the pleasure was soon at hand. What a welcoming way to begin the weekend?

I thought I could get very used to this type of greeting. We ordered food, and opened the wine, and cuddled up on the couch for the rest of the evening. For the first time, I thought this lady could be the "one". She made me feel special; was a great lover; and I totally enjoyed being in her company.

I knew Erin was only an on-again, off-again relationship. If I was really honest with myself; it was more **off** than **on**. I probably wouldn't break Erin's heart if I told her goodbye. Oh yes, maybe she might be a slight bit hurt that I had found someone else to replace her; but for the most part, that "hurt" would not last long.

On the other hand if I told Amy, I am sure she would have been heart-broken, because she was making plans for our future together. I am not saying that this loss would be tragic for Amy; but she would be more upset that her future and that of her kids would be shattered. I really liked Amy. She was generally fun to be around, a good lover, and willing to please. In hind-sight, if I had really thought this out as I am doing now, I have no idea how things might have worked out. But, I am getting way ahead of myself.

When Aerial and I went to bed later that Friday night, were we like a young married couple on their honeymoon night. We could not get enough sex to fill either of our desires. We had sex long into the early hours of the morning; until at last sleep overtook us. We fell into a total relaxed state of blissful sleep. It was mid Saturday afternoon when we both started to wake up. Aerial was doing her best to assist my rising. Soon, we were locked into love-making and sharing pleasure. What a satisfying a way to start the day. Aerial and I just lay there in each other's arms; neither of us wanting to get out of bed. So the day drifted by, until hunger for food made us head for the kitchen. Although it was late Saturday afternoon, Aerial made us breakfast of bacon and eggs, toast and coffee, and we were set for the day. Neither of us wanted to get dressed, just on the off chance that passion would arouse us. Both of us would be willing to comply; so we remained as we were for the balance of the day.

It was not till later that evening that sex would raise its desire; so the balance of the day and the evening were spent just lying around cuddled up on the couch watching TV. I thought to myself . . . this is what I have been waiting for . . . a relationship where only the two of us mattered. The rest of the world could just go merrily on its way. Both our sex drives must have been in a slow-down mode, because we only had a brief sexual encounter that night and soon we were asleep in each other's arms. Aerial again regained her interest in sex, as the early morning sun started to glow in the room. She was again on me and helping me rise to the occasion.

After making love again, Aerial said we couldn't stay in bed all day since she had laundry and ironing to do to get ready for Monday. She also had her nursing course notes to review for the test on Monday. Sadly, I acknowledged that I agreed with her. I asked if she wanted me to make some breakfast for her, she shook her head "no".

As I was getting dressed, a feeling of sadness fell came over me. I knew in my heart that I did not want to leave this lady, and the great weekend that we just had. I kissed her goodbye; told her we would talk through the week and make plans for our next time together. I told her that it had been a fantastic weekend, and I wanted to be with her again, very soon. I hoped she felt the same. We kissed again, and I left for my parent's home.

I was talking to myself all the way home and asked several times, *"Was I actually in love with this girl or was it just lust?"* I couldn't decide, and as I entered my parent's home, my mother just smiled, and said *"Have a good weekend Paul? I wished you had called to tell me you were not coming home, I was worried"*? I apologized, and told her that I really had a good weekend and I was very happy to have Aerial in my life.

I said to my mother, *"I understand you are having a test on Monday. I wish you good luck"*, and she just smiled in reply.

Monday was soon greeting me, and Amy was quick to get to my desk to inquire about my weekend and to tell me of hers. I pretended to seem interested in all that she was saying; but I just couldn't get Aerial out of my mind and the great weekend we'd shared. I told Amy l had to get busy and complete a report. As she walked away, she said *"See you at coffee break"*.

Fortunately, I did have to have a report done; so it was a good excuse to have a short coffee break with Amy. I busied myself with the task at hand, and soon the day was drawing to an end. Once more Amy was at my desk, asking to speak with me. She said *"Is it my imagination or are you avoiding me"*? I apologized and said it was just getting the report done and in on time, that had consumed all my attention.

This seemed to be a satisfactory response, and Amy then apologized to me, *"Sorry I just felt like things had changed between us or at least that is what I was feeling"*. I said *"No need to apologize"* and that I would talk to her later, since she had to get home to her kids.

On my drive home, I was fighting with myself about what I should do with this relationship with Amy. Should I end it or just go along for the ride and see where it went? I was in the early stages with Aerial, and I did not want to cut off Amy and good sex. If Aerial was not going to be available for awhile, and if the final major examination was coming up soon, that meant that Aerial would not be too available.

I did not want to put myself in a dry period of not being able to enjoy sex with either of them. Then I realized that Erin's friend Rebecca was still available for sex, if only Erin would be available for a date. Erin always put me last on the list of things to do. She had always told me that she did not want to have sex until we were married, so there would definitely be no action coming from that source. My options for sex would be limited; so I thought it best to hang onto Amy at least for the time being. I smiled and thought that I had reasoned that out quite well, and so the rest of the drive home did not seem quite so intense.

To my surprise I got a call from Erin on Monday night. She said that she had missed me and hoped that l had a good weekend. I told her that it was good seeing my old friend again, and asked how their weekend had been. Erin asked if I wanted to get together tonight and we could go for a drink. I told her that it would be great to see her and have some time together. After I hung up, I realized that I now had a problem. I was supposed to call Amy that night. What do I do? I called Amy and told her that I had a headache, probably stress from working on that report all day. I was sorry and could not talk any longer; but would see her tomorrow.

Amy was not pleased, and I sensed it in her tone of voice; but that was the best excuse I could give her. But I knew she would be at my desk early next day.

Erin and I actually had a very enjoyable evening, a few drinks, a few laughs, and even some good conversation about our relationship. She said *"I know you are not happy with me not being around much and spending more time with friends than with you. But I need this time for myself"*. I said I sort of understood where she was coming from; but I did feel left out and it did hurt not being included in her time with her friends. Erin just said *"Give me a little more time and space, till I get this restless spirit out of my system, and then it will be great for us"*. I was both happy and sad with this statement, because it meant very little time with her, or the possibility of sex with Rebecca. However, it also meant I would have the time to spend with Aerial and Amy both. It was a two-edged sword; but it was something that I could work with. It would be easier to juggle two women, rather than three. I told Erin that I would give her all the time she needed, and she was pleased.

When I dropped Erin at home, she even gave me a passionate kiss . . . something that we had not done in a long time, and again, she thanked me for my patience. On the drive home I thought, "well I might be a rat; but at least I was a logical rat" and I had made Erin happy for the moment and indeed my life was a little easier.

As I had suspected, Amy was at my desk first thing Tuesday morning. She said *"What is going on with you? Do you think I believe your story? I am not that gullible, buddy."* I smiled and said in the most convincing voice I could muster, that I **did** have a headache and I did **not** appreciate her statements. I must have come across as very sincere, and I kept a straight face. Amy said she was sorry that she had doubted me and asked for my forgiveness. I told her that I would forgive her, but do not accuse me like that in the future, or we would be done. I think that actual tears were forming in her eyes, and she excused herself and left my desk. Boy, what a performance I had just given. I turned the guilt from me to her and she felt badly. In reality, it was me who had been very bad.

I called Aerial Tuesday afternoon right after work just to see how her test had gone, and in general to ask about her whole day. Aerial said she was happy that I called and that she really had a good weekend with me and looked forward to more of the same with me. The next word out of her mouth is what stopped me dead in my speech. She would be busy studying for the upcoming examinations and we would have to be put on hold till they were over, and she hoped I understood.

I attempted to put forth my best "yes I understand", but Aerial jumped in the conversation and said *"Is there a problem what that or with us being together? You don't sound too convincing"*. I realized that it was my lower brain (my penis) speaking, not my head, so I quickly responded that it was just that I would miss her, but I honestly understood. Aerial said *"That is very sweet, to know you will miss me, but I will miss you as well. But my exams have to come first"*.

As I hung up, I realized that if I wanted sex, then there was only Amy left, so I had better smarten up. After supper that night, I called Amy and told her that I was sorry how I had acted, but that I was a little stressed out, and if I took it out on her, then I was sorry. Boy am I ever full of the `"old blarney". I should be on a tall tale game show, as I had to be quick-witted to come up with some of these reasonable stories. It was about this time that my stomach was bothering me, and I told my mom about the discomfort.

Mom said she would make an appointment with the doctor for an examination, to get to the source of the problem. When I went into the doctor's office, he asked some general comments about my health and what symptoms I had. The doctor asked if I had any problems at home, or at work that was causing stress to me. I replied that all was going well both on the home front and at work. The doctor asked if I was having any financial problems and I replied that there was no problem there as well. The doctor then asked if I had a girlfriend, and were we getting along. To this I replied *"Which girlfriend are you referring to"?*

The doctor asked *"How many girlfriends do you have"?* I replied that I had one girlfriend, but that I was also dating two other girls at the same time. The doctor told me that I had the beginning of an ulcer, and to get rid of the two girlfriends, that all would improve and to get the hell out of his office.

I guess the doctor did not have any sense of humour, or likely as a professional, he knew that the problem was my own doing, and he was not impressed with my taking up his valuable time.

Wednesday morning Amy was at my desk again, but this time with a big smile on her face. She told me as a make-up between us that she would buy coffee this morning. I quickly gave a smile in return, and said *"I will be looking forward to break-time with you, and you buying makes it all the better"*. Then I laughed a hearty laugh and she was gone. At coffee break she said *"I want to make it up to you, for doubting you and our relationship, so come for supper tonight"*. I told her that I would love to come over and that I would call Mom and let her know that I would not be home for supper.

When I arrived at Amy's I was again in a different world. Her kids were there, yelling at each other and Amy was trying to calm the uproar and go about making supper preparations. I knew instantly that this would not be something that I would not like to sign on for the long-term arrangement. It was different again, at the supper table. Amy asked about her kids' day at school. They asked why I was there for supper, and also told about the upcoming events and the supplies they needed for it.

It was not a pleasant supper time for me; but I tried to react to the situation in a positive way. I knew that if I blew this supper time that any sex that I was hoping for, would not be forthcoming. Amy said that she thought the dinner time with me and her kids went well. What did I think? I quickly put my brain in overdrive. My response would be a make or break situation. I told her that it was a new experience (no lie yet); but that all in all it was not so bad. Now, this was a lie! Amy smiled and said *"I am glad you thought that way, because my kids are very important to me"*. I now knew that I had passed with flying colours, and all was well on the home front.

Amy told me that after the kids went to bed, it would be our time, and promised me I would not be disappointed. Time with the kids, the TV programs, getting them ready for bed . . . all seemed to take an eternity. At long last, the little "monsters" were in bed and my time was at hand.

Amy told me that I would have to have patience, because we had to wait till the kids were asleep. As we watched TV, I became a little frisky, my hands started to roam over her breasts, down her legs; the passion pulse was beating fast. Just as I was getting super-turned-on, the "pitter-patter" of little feet coming down the stairs brought things to an instant halt.

The joy of children, (humbug) was my first gut reaction. Then her son was in the room complaining about the noise of the TV. Amy and I had been totally unaware of its sound, since we were getting in the mood for the pleasure to follow. Amy took her son upstairs to his bedroom, came down and turned down the TV. There we sat, the moment of passion once begun, was now totally starting to consume us. Amy said *"We will have to be quiet for a bit, to see that they are asleep, before we can go upstairs"*. We waited for close to two hours, simply sitting on the couch, holding hands, like a first date and waiting for total quiet from upstairs.

Finally, Amy and I headed upstairs, the sexual drive in me was strong, and Amy was more than willing to comply. I thought the sounds of the bed hitting the wall would have awakened either the neighbours next door, or her kids. But that thought quickly fled as our ride of passion went into overdrive.

It was late night/early morning when I rose from the bed to head for my parent's home; had a brief sleep period, and then went back to work. I thought that yes the love-making was fantastic; but having to wait for her kids to go to sleep was not pleasurable. I guess you have to take the good with the bad; but I knew I could not handle this type of arrangement all week long. It would have to be weekend pleasure only, for this lad.

My stomach problems were indeed easing off, so the doctor must have been correct . . . only one woman at a time. It seemed to be working out well at the moment. Both Erin and Aerial were indisposed. Amy was happy and this gave me a very satisfying sex life. Time marched on; all was peaceful. So I became unaware that school exams were drawing to a close.

Aerial called that Thursday evening, to tell me that she wanted to get together with me. *"What are we going to do this weekend?"* I told her that I would call Friday after work to see what plans we could make for the weekend. I should have paid more attention at home. My mother had told me she was glad to be done with exams; but I had not paid a great deal of attention. I was about to get into hot water again! If only I could have sex with the both of them on the weekend. Where was their sense of humour?

I realized that this was only a dream, not reality. So, what was I going to do? I knew that I would have to go out with Aerial, especially to celebrate the end of examinations. Besides that, we hadn't had sex with each other for awhile. It could be a wild weekend of pleasure for both of us. My only problem was what to do with Amy.

I thought that since she had gone away with her parents and her kids for the weekend, I had to understand the situation. I just had to come up with a good reason why I was going to be busy this weekend. Logically, I was on the right road of not being available.

But what would be the reason? I told Amy that my Mother had just finished her examinations, since Amy knew that she was in the nursing course from our previous conversation. I told her that Dad had surprised Mom with tickets to see the Phantom of the Opera in Toronto to celebrate the end of exams and had bought me a ticket as well. I really did like live theatre, and had told Amy that before. Consequently, that part of the story was true.

When I told Amy of my weekend plans, she asked me why I was going along. I said that Dad thought it would be nice if we had a "family getaway" since we had all been part of the exam process. Mom had the exams and Dad and I did the housework and looked after meal preparation. Amy fell for this . . . hook, line, and sinker. Even I believed the story; it sounded that believable.

I called Aerial Friday right after work and said *"Honey I am all yours."* and she just laughed in response. We chatted for a brief time, and Aerial said *"What are you waiting for; get on over here, so we can begin the weekend"*. I was eager to comply, and I threw a kiss in the air to Mom, and said *"I probably won't be home tonight or possibly for the whole weekend?"*

Mom just smiled her knowing smile, and I was out the door and on my way to Aerial's apartment. She greeted me at the doorway, wearing only her housecoat, which she flashed open to expose her nude body. Aerial said *"See anything your like big boy?"*, and with that she was helping me undress, and walked me to her bedroom.

We were like animals in heat, tugging here, pulling there to get me nude, so that our bodies could be locked in ecstasy. I forgot what wild, fulfilling sexual pleasure that Aerial was capable of, and how turned on she could get me.

We laid there in total exhaustion . . . both of us in a pool of sweat, our breathing heavy, my pleasure meter still ticking, but unable to speak or able to move. It was now early evening and both of us were hungry. We decided to call for a pizza, to build up or strength, on the off chance that we may become consumed with one another again.

When we went to bed that night, we both fell into a heavy sleep right away, because our pleasure was still registering full.

Saturday, we were like a young married couple, helping strip the bed, doing the laundry, as well as making breakfast together. Saturday was a lazy, laid-back kind of a day, but I told Aerial we should make plans to go to for dinner and a show, to celebrate the end of exams.

Aerial said *"That would be great, and do I get to choose both the restaurant and show"*? I told her that this was her celebration, and of course it would be totally her choice. We made reservations for supper and then proceeded to look together through the paper for the show and the time that Aerial wanted.

I thought I could get used to this life style. It all seemed too perfect. However, I felt the uneasy "hammer of change" must soon follow. When we returned to Aerial's apartment, I knew something was wrong. She seemed to be very serious, so I sat down and waited. Aerial opened a bottle of wine; poured us each a glass, and said *"I need to tell you something, so please sit down"*. For a split second, the thought that raced through my mind even seared me. I thought she was going to say that she was pregnant, or that she had met someone else, or that there had always been someone else, and he had now returned.

None of that was the case, as I was just about to find out. Aerial said she had accepted a job position at a hospital in Chatham. Her marks were excellent and all had gone well. She told me she would be starting there after the graduation ceremonies, which were next weekend. My first reaction was to say "congratulations" . . . which I did. Then I said *"what about us?"* Aerial said that when she had time off, she would call and that I could come down and spend time with her. I said *"Yes, but with shift work, it could be difficult to have many weekends together."*

Aerial said she realized that, but thought that a little time apart would make the heart grow fonder, and we would really enjoy the time together when it happened. I said to her that I really enjoyed the time we had together right now. It was perfect! Why change things? Aerial said that she wanted to get married, and that she wanted us both to be sure that it was love between us, not just lust.

I was totally taken aback with this discussion. I did not want to stop the system of pleasure that I had in place; but I did feel something for this lady. But was it enough to change my ways? We made small talk for the balance of the night, and went to bed. We shared a kiss, rolled over, each of us not wanting to start a quarrel and finally went to sleep.

When Sunday morning finally arrived, we gave each other a good morning kiss, and rolled out of bed. There was no cuddling, no friskiness. We just simply got up. This was our first disagreement, and I did not like the feeling one little bit. I thought to myself; was I being selfish wanting her to get a job nearby, or was she testing me and my willingness to come to her when she beckoned?

I was already in that kind of relationship with Erin and she had me on hold till she got in the mood. I wasn't looking for a second "cup of control" over me and my comings and goings. We made our own individual breakfasts, drank our coffee and read the morning paper, all in silence. I told her that I was sorry for the way the weekend ended, gave her a kiss goodbye and said that I would talk to her later.

I didn't talk with her later that day. Instead I did a lot of thinking about the direction in which Aerial was forcing me. I knew from just driving home from Amy's home in London to St. Thomas, in the early morning hours, how tired I was next day at work. How in the world would I be able to drive home from Chatham through the week and still go to work the next day? I knew that this was the beginning of the end of our relationship. I was convinced it would not work out for either of us.

Monday morning, Amy was at my desk asking a million and one questions about my weekend. Fortunately for me a fellow employee at work was actually going to see the Phantom of the Opera, and that was where my idea had come from. I had even read his programme of information about it, and the tour he was going on. So, I was very knowledgeable, and could easily answer any and all questions correctly. I told Amy that the graduation ceremonies were this coming weekend and after that I would be all hers. She was sad, but then she realized it was only one more weekend without me, and then all would resume back to normal with us. I called Aerial mid-week and told her that I was sorry and did not want to see our relationship end. I was sweet as sugar because if I thought it was over, then it should end in a bang, literally.

Aerial said she would forgive me and that Friday night I should plan on spending the weekend with her. She said *"Since you are taking me to my graduation tell your Mom and Dad to save seats beside them.*

Then the four of us will be together." I told her that I was looking forward to being with her again; that I missed her, and all the good times we shared. I did not want to make her unhappy, and I did like cuddling with her and having her in my arms.

Boy, I thought to myself, if I was a girl, I would have believed this line of mush myself!! Friday night was finally here. It seemed like a long week; but I guess when one anticipates a weekend, the week seems to drag. I called Aerial and asked her what time she wanted me to come over. Perhaps she would like to go out for dinner, to help set things right between us. Aerial said she thought that it was be very nice to have a romantic dinner and maybe a walk along Port Stanley beach afterwards in the moonlight. We could talk, hug, and hold one another, like we used to.

I thought this could definitely set the mood for a good, fun-filled weekend of pleasure. We followed Aerial's plans to a "T". I was also scheming to find a way to make love on the beach, as though it "just came naturally" in the moment. As we were kissing and hugging on the beach, the moonlight was streaming over the lake, as though it were a walkway to the other side.

I made my move. I started to run my hands over her buttocks, then move ever so slowly upwards over her breasts, all the while, kissing her passionately, on the lips, cheeks and the back of her neck. I knew from past experiences, that this kiss on the neck was the thing that most turned her on.

Aerial said *"Make love to me; I miss you; I need you, take me"*. With that we were on the sand and our bodies were locked in ecstasy. My plan had worked out quite well. Round one done; round two later. When we returned to Aerial's apartment, I had planned that when she went in the shower to get the sand off her body, I would join her. As though she had read my mind, Aerial headed for the shower with me in hot pursuit.

She had just removed her clothes, turned on the water, and was heading in. In a heartbeat I was nude and standing behind her. Aerial smiled and said *"You are either very horny, or you really missed me"*. I responded the *"I missed you honey"*. We had not had sex in the shower for quite awhile, and I had forgotten how wonderful a sensation it was. That was a very good, well thought-out plan, and I was proud of myself how well it had come together.

Friday night was indeed worth the money I had spent, to receive the pleasures of the body that I did enjoy. If this was to be my last weekend with Aerial, I was going to make love to her many times, in many ways, so that the lasting memories would leave its mark. Saturday morning was again a pleasurable way to start the day. Aerial said *"Are you on energy pills or what? I cannot believe your sex drive! It's in overdrive!"* I told her I was making up for last weekend since we had a bit of a drought . . . no sex Saturday or Sunday.

Aerial said *"You poor boy. When I am not happy, then you are not going to be happy either."* and I just smiled and said *"Yes I know, and I will try and behave".* It was afternoon before we started to get dressed to go to her graduation ceremonies. She looked beautiful in her new dress, like a princess I thought. We met my parents as they arrived in the parking lot at the same time. I kissed my Mom, and told her she looked beautiful as well. The four of us strolled towards the assembly hall.

I was very proud of my mother; she was the oldest graduate on the stage and she actually won an award for the highest passing grade of all the graduates. There were refreshments and goodies being served after the ceremonies, and lots of picture-taking of graduates, parents, and their significant others. It was a wonderful day and the weather co-operated as well. Everyone had smiles and the atmosphere was all consuming.

My parents, Aerial and I had decided to go to dinner together. Things were getting very thick between my parents and Aerial and I was feeling a little uneasy. I knew this was our last weekend and my parents and Aerial were acting like this was our engagement night. Horrors of horrors! Slow down people.

It really was a lovely night with Aerial and Mom sharing stories of school, their hard work to graduate, their future jobs, and getting finally in the workforce. I was kind of sorry to see the night end; but all things do come to an end, whether you are ready or not. Soon we departed for our separate homes.

Saturday night as we undressed each other, we each felt like this was our honeymoon night. Slowly, taking each other's clothes off, we smiled; each of us anticipating making love. I guess it was because of the dinner with my parents, that this feeling had come over the both of us. As we slid into bed, the shyness disappeared. We went into a frenzy of winding our bodies around one another, and soon we were locked together. What a fantastic way to wrap up the day, and thoughts of tomorrow morning danced in my head as we kissed good night and drifted into welcoming sleep.

Sunday morning and Aerial was helping me rise to the occasion, and soon we were into heavy, passionate, love-making, as if there were no ending. We were laying there, both of us breathing heavily and sweating. The thought that this could be my last love-making with Aerial overcame me and a few seconds of sorrow followed. I knew at the end of this day, that our relationship would be through; but I took great delight in knowing that I would have many memories of this lovely lady and the pleasure that she could bestow.

She had such beauty within that drew you to her, and she evoked such a strong desire to have her. I thought that either I did love her, or would shortly, if the job location had been different. I think my happiness would have been found; but young and foolish, I let her slip without giving it a second thought. If I could only turn back the hands of time, to undo the mistakes I had made in my life. IF ONLY! IF ONLY!!

Monday and Amy appeared at my desk with big smile, saying *"Let's go for a walk on our coffee break"*. I was a little concerned with this comment. Was something up between us? Was she going to lay down the law, or was it just a simple walk, talk, and time to be together?

I was in suspense until the coffee-break hour, a little unsure of the fate that awaited me. Amy came to get me at the appointed hour and said *"Ready to go big boy?"* With that comment, all my worrying passed, because I knew then, that everything was "OK" in my world. We walked slowly and Amy was asking questions about the graduation ceremonies. Did my mother get a dress for the occasion? How many people graduated? I was not sure if she was really interested or whether she was just checking to see if I did attend the day and evening celebrations. The questions were coming fast and furious and I did not have much time to think of the answer. So I realized I was being tested. Luckily for me I had a double reason to attend.

My mother's big day and with Aerial in the same graduation class made it a very unique situation. Consequently, I would have been there regardless of the circumstances. Amy told me how she had missed me, and she hoped that we would be spending this coming weekend together. She said that it had been a long, quiet weekend with just her kids around, and she longed for my company.

I told her that indeed we could make plans for this weekend and any following weekend because I was all hers. Amy grabbed for my hand and gave it a little squeeze, and a smile of pleasure came over her face. I looked at my watch and told her we had better get back to the office. We had over-stayed the fifteen minute break time and I knew that the manager's eyes would be glaring when we returned.

When I got to my desk, I thought, well Aerial is long gone. Erin hadn't called; so the last resort was Amy for any future sexual gratification. I really did not want to get back into this relationship. The kids were a pain, but Amy was here, and the pleasure meter was ticking. I thought I could handle this for a little while. If need be, I would bail out and look at some other possibilities. Perhaps Erin might come to her senses.

Friday night finally arrived and I had told Amy that I would take her out to dinner and a show; but she said she had no babysitter. Could we do it on Saturday instead? I guess the kids threw a curve into our plans; I had not had to worry about that for the last two weeks. Welcome back to reality.

Amy told me she still wanted me to come over and we would just watch TV Friday night. When I arrived at Amy's home, she and her kids were just sitting outside on the porch. She told the kids they could play outside a little longer. Then it would be time to come in. She invited me in and got me a glass of wine. We could talk till the kids came in.

We made small talk about everything under the sun. Then the kids were there, sitting down in the room with us. Their curiosity had gotten the better of them. Oh joy, we four were going to watch TV together! I could hardly contain myself. Welcome to the "family life". Amy sensed my uneasiness, and asked if there was anything wrong. I told her that I just did not like the show that her kids were watching. She smiled and said *"Just have patience; they will be going to bed soon"*. If I had said *"I really do not like having your kids around us"*, then my stay would have been short lived and I would be on my way home.

Soon it was time for her kids to go to bed. It was already 10:30 p.m. and the night was fading away quickly. Amy still had to get them settled for the night. I started to wonder if Amy herself had gone to bed, because it seemed to be taking a long time for her to return.

To my surprise when she reappeared, she was wearing a soft green, see-through nightie, and she asked *"See any thing that you like?* I grabbed her towards me on the couch; my manhood had already risen to attention. I said *"I missed you, I need you and I want you, now"!* Amy smiled and replied that she was glad I had missed her and she said *"It definitely shows. See what going without sex is like? You will appreciate me more."* Then she giggled and we were lost in the moment. How long we were locked together was a total unknown; but who was watching time. My pleasure meter was working overtime. We both were eventually totally satisfied and rolled over on the couch, remaining entwined in each other's arms.

We smiled at one another and then she said *"I could make you this happy and fulfilled all your life. You would never be this horny ever".* I replied that she had a few tricks up her sleeve that did send me into a state of utter exhaustion and contentment, and I loved having sex with her.

Amy smiled happily, knowing that the pleasure she had given me had indeed locked our relationship. She felt secure as well as her future had been established. Amy asked *"Are you going to stay the rest of the night"?* I replied that I had things to do on Saturday, but that maybe Saturday night I might stay. I dressed and headed for the doorway, gave Amy a parting kiss, and I was off to my parent's home.

On my drive home it suddenly occurred to me what Amy had said about having no sex for a couple of weeks. Hell, I was always this horny, and I smiled contentedly, knowing full well, that I had not gone without sex for two weeks, but that would remain my little secret.

I called Amy mid-afternoon to see if our plans for a dinner and show were still on for that night. Amy said she was happy that I had called and yes we could still go out that night. I asked her if she had any place in mind for dinner. She replied she would like to go to the Keg restaurant for a romantic dinner, and that a show didn't really matter. I asked what time I should arrive and when the babysitter was coming. I could synchronize my timing, and then we could leave when I arrived. Everything worked out and soon after I arrived, we were on our way to the restaurant.

The atmosphere was very romantic with dim lights, candles on the table, soft music playing in the back ground, and the wine on arrival was chilled to perfection. Amy looked very attractive. We had decided to "dress" for the evening, and her low neckline, black, tight fitting dress, left nothing to the imagination. A lady was walking around selling roses from her basket, and I purchased a long stem red rose to add to the perfect evening we were planning.

After our delicious dinner, I ordered specialty coffees for us to enjoy. The hour was getting late and the perfect evening was drawing to an end. Soon we would be heading to Amy's. My expectations of further pleasures were dancing in my head, as we drove home.

When we arrived at Amy's, she told me to pay the babysitter. I did not think I should have to; but I complied as directed, and soon we were alone. Amy thanked me and told me she had limited funds left till payday. Then she said *"This is how it is done now, when you have a date"*. She sensed I was not pleased, and said *"All right I will pay in the future; don't get mad"*.

The bells should have been ringing again, at this display of her emotions; but I was not working with my brain at this stage. Amy asked if I wanted another drink, and I declined, saying *"I was ready for bed and sleep"*. Sleep was indeed the order of the evening since too much alcohol had been consumed. With full bellies, sleep soon overtook both of us.

What a strange dream I was having. But in reality, it was no dream. Amy's son walked into the bedroom and told his mother he was hungry and wanted his breakfast. What the hell was going on? I finally came to my senses and realized where I was. Welcome to family life! I got up, had my shower, got dressed, and stumbled down the staircase to where Amy sat alone.

The kids had already had their breakfast and had gone outside to play. Amy made coffee and was smiling at me as I came into the kitchen. Amy said *"Rough night, last night. Are you going to survive"?*

I asked her how she felt, and she replied *"I feel a little rough but obviously not as bad as you look"*, and she laughed and told me to sit down. She said she was a little surprised how quickly we went to sleep. Then she laughed again and said *"that was the first time we went to bed and didn't have sex"*.

Amy poured the badly needed coffee and asked if I wanted something to eat. I told her that toast would be great, and then I set about having some coffee. Probably an hour later, I was actually feeling human again, and asked her what her plans were for the day. She told me that she had laundry and ironing to do but there no rush for me to go and I could stay for awhile and keep her company. I was in no particular hurry to get home, so I settled in. Amy poured another coffee, and then she was off to the basement to do the laundry.

Amy told me to go, make myself comfortable in the living room, turn on the TV and that she would join me shortly to do some ironing. It was not long and she was setting up to do the job at hand . . . all the while she was smiling.

Amy told me that this weekend had been really nice, and what did I think of it? I asked what she meant, and she replied that this was the first time I had stayed over and started the day with her and her kids. I said it was a different experience. Then she stared at me. I continued saying that it was nice having you by my side and to wake up with you.

Her kids early morning schedule was a different thing. I thanked God that I had continued talking or my name would have been mud. My brain had enough caffeine to finally kick into gear, so the rest of my statement was my salvation. Amy smiled and I knew that my quick response was a good one. I had to be on my toes just on the off chance there would be more questions. Questions indeed were to follow . . . a steady, endless stream that seemed and yet somehow did clear the air of any misunderstandings between us.

Amy had now entered into the second phase of her plan. Amy put it right on the line, *"Do you love me; do you want me in your life; and when are you going to make a commitment to that effect?"* I had no room to manoeuvre. A straight forward answer had to be given and given now. I told Amy, that I did love her, and did want her in my life. I told her I was not sure when I could make a commitment; but I would work on that one. I thought that while Amy was finally quiet (maybe a bad sign or possibly a good sign) I had better get the hell out of there and take a really good look at the whole picture. I needed time I told Amy and she replied *"You had better not come back here until you can make a firm commitment, and mean it, buster".*

On the drive home, my brain seemed to be going in a thousand different directions. My reasoning powers seemed to be functioning because it all started to make sense. The whole picture was right in front of my face. I seemed to be happy. Was this love? Was this what I had been looking for?

I knew it was not necessarily someone with a ready-made family, but maybe that would not be a big deal. The sex was great. She had been taken on full time at work; so there would be an additional income. In reality there was no one else on the scene. I felt Erin had dumped me; but she had yet to tell me. I was getting older; I wanted a soul-mate. I wanted to belong to someone and for someone to belong to me. I would give it a little time, and see what might come of it. The only thought that was constant was that there would be no sex for a while. How long a drought period lay ahead?

Work on Monday seemed strange with no Amy at my desk. There were no questions, no good morning smile; no "see you later" comments. It was just a void full of silence, an un-natural start for the day. Coffee break seemed strange as well. Amy was sitting with the girls from the office and I was searching for a table of guys to share time with. I did not enjoy this much, and even eye contact with Amy was cold and un-feeling.

As I passed Amy at her desk after the morning coffee, I said "good morning Amy" and she of course did not reply. It was as though I had not spoken a word. To call the whole situation that I was now currently in an "ice box" would barely scratch the surface. The week proceeded very much as it had started. Not one word was spoken between us, and it was going to be a very long, non-eventful weekend.

My mother realized that something must be up because mothers are very tuned in to their kids. She asked if I wanted to talk about what was going on in my life. I told her what Amy had said to me the weekend before, and being a good mother she said *"Son you had better do some serious thinking. This is your life and your happiness that you are considering."* I thanked her and retired to my room, to do just that. It soon appeared that no quick answer was evident. A long battle within me was just getting started.

All weekend I was consumed with this issue, and got no sleep at all. My mind was not willing to shut down.

It was soon Monday and I was told by many fellow employees that I looked pale. Was I feeling okay? Amy rushed by my desk, made a brief stop, told me I looked terrible, and was off to her own work station. In hindsight, I wondered if she was pleased that I looked terrible. From my perspective, she looked good.

I have been told that women like to see a man squirm, when they have the upper hand. They like to sit back and wait for the end result. Women can play this game so well that no man has a chance. He is doomed but just does not know it yet. It is like the old philosophy, "too soon old, too late smart".

Two more weeks rolled by. I still didn't have an answer about when I can make a commitment, or even if I wanted one. I am really looking a mess. My dear mother was even starting to wonder about the state of my health and bluntly told me *"Either shit or get off the pot"*.

I thought enough is enough; let's give it a try. What is the worst thing that can happen? I would later eat these words and it will eventually become very transparent at a later stage in this story.

On Monday morning, again Amy brushed against my desk, stopped and looked at me for a second and then started to head towards her work station. As she was leaving, I said *"Amy I have made a decision"*, and she stopped dead in her tracks. She returned to my desk, and said *"Well what have you to say for yourself?"* and I told her that I wanted her and the whole nine yards.

An ear to ear smile beamed and she said *"Let's walk together on our coffee break, ok honey?"* and with that she was off. I was amazed at the transformation. It was like night and day in an instant. And now I was "honey", not just an object in a chair. They say there is nothing like a woman's scorn, and I had been the receiver of such treatment. Now I am smart enough to know I did not want it again.

The coffee break was soon at hand, and with a big smile Amy was waltzing to my desk and saying *"Ready to go honey?"* It was as though the sunshine had returned after many weeks of cloud and storm. A very welcome change in conditions and atmosphere was now present.

As we were walking, Amy grabbed my hand and said *"I have missed you so much, and I am so glad we are going to start a life together"*. I told Amy that I too had missed her. Sex was at the head of the line and I was glad we would be starting our relationship again. I took things slowly at the beginning, not wanting her to know how horny I was, and I was content with hand holding and kissing. This seemed to please her that I was not demanding sex right away, but was just happy to just be with her. I thought that I had better use a little psychology to win her over. This plan of mine seemed to be doing the trick. She was feeling secure in our relationship and our future, and finally she blurted out to me *"Are you not horny? I sure am. Let's have sex tonight"*.

I said *"Sounds like a plan. I thought you'd never ask."* With that being said, I enjoyed a belly laugh. I wondered momentarily, if I had hung on to this game of Amy's a little longer, would I have indeed been the winner? This I would never know, but the second question I had to ask was this. Would I have been able to have the will power to do so? Thirdly if I was honest with myself, the sex drought was indeed over, and I took pleasure in that thought rather than in Amy winning. Amy and I were back again as a happy couple; the world was turning in its proper rotation, the moon at night, and sun in the day. All was as it should be.

One day while on our coffee break walk, Amy told me she had been given an opportunity to go this weekend to a woman's weekend conference, sponsored by work. What did I think about the idea? I tried not to react too hastily, but wanted to respond more slowly, so that it would sound genuine and sincere.

I told Amy that it would be great idea to attend; it was a free weekend away. She would learn additional skills, and it could lead to either a new job offer or a different pay level. All of these were positives to going. Amy was very happy with my thoughts and told me that was what she had been thinking. I shouldn't go there; you know with "the devil put me up to this line". If she had indeed been able to rationally come up with this thought on her own, then there would have been two moons in the sky that night. I just could not in all honesty let that slip by!! My positive thinking and encouragement of the idea easily swung Amy over to going. She was high on the idea, and could not wait to go.

In the back of my mind, I had a different reason for applying my logic to the posed question. I thought I would give Aerial a call out of the blue; just on the off chance there might be some interest. If not, at least I took the opportunity when it availed itself. After all, it was only one weekend without sex at the worst.

I called Aerial that very afternoon after work, and luck of the Irish, she was at home. Aerial said *"I am both very surprised and happy to hear your voice. How are you and what's up with the call"?* I told her that I was just thinking of her, wondering how things were going. I also told her how I missed her smile. This was usually a good response that might have favourable results. I asked her if she was going to be free this weekend. I would like to come down and take her out to dinner. Aerial told me that she was just finishing her afternoon shift and would be home Friday at 3:30 p.m. She told me she had Saturday off; but would have to go in to work Sunday night. She asked me when I thought that I might be coming down. I told her I thought she probably had weekend plans or things that needed to be done. Probably Friday would be best, and then I would not keep her back from any other plans.

Aerial said that would be great to see me and get caught up on each other's life. I asked her how to get to her apartment in Chatham and she described the route in detail. I told her I would come down right after work, to expect me by 6:00 p.m. and we could go right to supper. She could pick the spot because I had no clue where we might go. I ended the conversation with, *"I am looking forward to seeing you. Enjoy the rest of the week."*

As the rest of the week whittled away, Amy said *"You seem mighty happy"*. I replied *"I am only happy for you, honey"*. You have not been away on your own for quite a while, and I think this will really make you happy and allow you to have an enjoyable time. This seemed to have done the trick. Amy was convinced that I had good intentions. My personal intentions were really good and so all was good between us. Friday at quitting time Amy and I said our farewell in the office parking lot. I told her I would call her Sunday and that I would miss her. That statement was mandatory and had to be said, to maintain good will between us, and keep my world intact. I had already had my car packed with some clothing; like a good boy scout I was prepared. I was Chatham bound. It was under a two hour drive to Aerial's building and I was there before 6:00 p.m. Here again I had to be crafty and not carry a suitcase to the door. It would be too obvious what my intentions were. So bare handed, I approached her apartment door. Aerial opened the door, threw her arms around me and planted a big kiss on my lips. What a nice welcome. I was totally unprepared for that. I was not sure what the response would be, and thought I might have to put a little work into the first kiss. But I was nicely fooled. Aerial invited me in, poured me a glass of wine, and then pointed me towards her living room. I said *"How about a small tour first?"* and she lead the way. It was a fairly large one bedroom apartment, and the floor plan had a nice flow to it. Aerial had decorated it very tastefully.

Aerial opened her bedroom door, and said "Excuse the mess; I have not been home too long, because I stopped to buy us a bottle of wine". Then Aerial laughed and said *"You have seen my bedroom a mess before; but you were never interested in that. The only thought you had was just getting me into bed "*. We both had a good laugh over that. But I thought, you're right; getting you into bed is on my mind. We walked back into the living room.

We talked non-stop for close to an hour, and then she noticed the time. She said *"We had better go, as they close up this small town early"*, and with that we were heading toward the door.

We headed for a quaint little restaurant that Aerial obviously had been to before. It had low lighting, soft music in the background, great food and we settled in for a most romantic evening. Soft words flowed between us; the connection to one another had been resurrected in this brief moment of time.

As we left the restaurant Aerial stopped me, pulled me close to her and pressed her lips on mine. This was followed by a few more moments of total union. Aerial said *"I want you to stay the night. Take me home and make love to me."* I was most willing to oblige, and indeed this had been my mission from the get go. Everything was going according to plan and I was beaming on the inside.

Getting ready to drive home, Aerial was caressing my body, kissing my neck, and basically exciting me to the point where driving the car was almost impossible. It was not long before lust overtook the both of us and soon we were caressing each other's body in the parking lot. Because the windows were fogging up quickly, the excitement was reaching a peak. We hastily sped home; got out of the car and into her place and the waiting bed of passion.

We made love throughout the night, just like a couple on their honeymoon. The night all too soon became morning, and as sleep was not over, we laid in each other arms, beamed at one another and then embraced.

This was the beginning of the morning pleasure routine that we had so often enjoyed in the past. Our bodies were hungry, lusting for more pleasure from our connection. We made love again before we both dozed off for a short nap. We resumed making love well into midmorning. Aerial said *"I had better get you some nourishment, if we are going to make love again".* I replied *"I am in no hurry to leave you or stop making love with you, unless you are running out of steam."* Then we both laughed out loud. My full intention was to not lose the moment or the contentment that was totally consuming us.

We both somehow knew that this was our final fling with one another. Different lives for us would now happen, from this point on and that we would have to return to the world of reality. We each knew we WOULD say our final good-byes to one another. We each knew that the memories of this weekend together would remain in our minds. There would be no more phone calls, no more pleasure weekends, not even penpals. This was the FINAL end for us!

And so late Sunday morning, after our final union, Aerial was off to work and the new life path she had chosen. I returned home. I had to bid farewell to Aerial, to our great sex, and possibly the makings of a good life together, to go to an unknown world where children would be a part of my life. My gut and my brain were not sure of this "uncertain" life that I had chosen with the possibility of many speed bumps to come.

I knew the distance to travel to Aerial's home, and her refusal to return to London to seek employment was a major problem. Yet I was so uncertain that the unknown world I had chosen was the right thing to do. This was a fine time to be thinking that way as I had obviously made a decision. My fate awaited me. I called Amy that night, trying desperately to sound happy to hear her voice. However, a silent voice within me was *saying "Are you really sure that you know what you are doing?"* Amy had a never ending flow of conversation, which was a good thing, as that meant all I had to do was listen. I could simply say "that's great" or "fantastic" or even a simple "yes" now and then. I don't think that Amy even detected that my heart was not in the conversation. But suddenly she said *"Are you not coming over to see me tonight"?*

My interest was very much peaked, and possibly making love might have been the pill to cure my state of mind. Amy greeted me at the door with a see-through purple nightie and told me the children were asleep. So bed was the place to go. As I was always in the mood for a play session, I quickly followed her upstairs for a roll in the hay, and to get my state of mind on the new course of life that was now was before me.

Amy seemed to notice a small lack of interest on my part. I guess I was still thinking of Aerial and the weekend with her; but quickly dropped that thought, and told Amy that I couldn't believe that I was with her again and I had missed her. The reality that I was now with her again had now totally settled in and this seemed to please her and bring back the desire to make passionate love again. She said *"I have missed you too."* It was near midnight when I crawled from her bed to head for my car and home. I knew all too well, that on Monday Amy would he pushing for a marriage date.

I was not wrong. I could have almost set my watch to the hour that the questions would flow. Amy walked by my desk as usual, smiled and said we would talk on our coffee break and she was again off to her work station. Had I only followed my gut instinct and run like hell, I would have missed this unpleasant time of my life.

I was and had only been using my small brain below instead of the one on my shoulders; so my fate was sealed, or so I thought. Again the thought or word '"retreat" never entered the larger brain and the blessed day was set for our union. Plans were set in motion, guest lists were being prepared. Costs were being discussed between her father and me. Happiness was the tone of the day. What a pink cloud I was in.

The marriage date was at hand, and that very day I had a surprise visit from Erin. She begged me to call it off, that she would marry me and to please come to my senses before the marriage happened. I told her it was too late to stop the marriage and that she was too late in taking an interest in my life. Had she not left me hanging all those times to find things to do with other people, I may not have been at this present stage in my life. In hindsight she was doing me a favour but I just couldn't see it at the moment. I told her that it was just a little too late to be offering to share my life.

A rejected Erin left, but not without instilling doubt about what I was about to do, a decision that was about to change my life.

My best man Jim arrived just as Erin was leaving. So I got the questions about why Erin was here, and what the hell was I doing. I told him that Erin had asked me to call off the wedding and that now I was not sure what I wanted to do with my life. Jim told me to forget her even being here. He added he was ready to party and for me not to upset everyone. I should just go through with the plans.

I said *"Let's go for a drink and discuss it some more."* We arrived at the bar, ordered our drinks and then the questions began. As we discussed Erin's visit and her wanting me in her life, he just laughed at that. *"Now she can't have you, she wants you, but for how long?"* I told Jim that I truly was having second thoughts about marriage, children and the life I would be getting into.

Jim again stated that he came to party and partying he intended to do at my wedding, so *"Suck it up and welcome to married life".* Here again, I should have just given Jim some money to drink and party with those in the bar and totally forget the marriage. He made me feel like I would be letting a lot of people down; that Erin had only shaken my thought process; that marriage would be good for me, and it was time for me to settle down. This was all very logical, and reasonable. The normal process would follow. But my gut was telling to run like hell!

The marriage took place. All the planning came together. People seemed happy, and a good time was had by all . . . except for me. The doubt existed within my whole been.

Amy had lived at a low income/subsidized housing townhouse which should have been a clue to me; but my upper brain had not been used well, before we were married. Purchasing the house and the financial cost for the wedding had drained my bank account. I was forced to return to work on Monday morning with NO honeymoon. Amy had to return as well since she had no money either. The normal routine of life continued, except it had felt like just a "party" weekend. In reality I would be going home with this woman from now on.

From the very beginning it felt very unnatural having kids at the supper table, supervising homework projects, reading bedtime stories, helping with housework, before sex or not. Then we had to rise to start the next day of the same routine. I thought we were instantly turned into an "old couple". Where had all the good times gone? This was far too serious a life style for me, at this time of my life!!

I had not really been aware of her kids. Generally when I arrived at her home, the kids were off to bed or in bed. So this had not been a huge part of my routine. I was totally unprepared for this. They came first and I was now number three in line for her attentions. Boy what a rude awakening for me! Along with many other little details, the "duties" she did for her kids, I realized that she only wanted a better life for herself and her kids. I was the instrument selected to obtain that goal.

My gut had been right!! As the slogan goes "A SUCKER IS BORN EVERY MINUTE" and I am "he".

I got a second job at a local clothing store, to be able to have time away from Amy's kids. It also gave me a little freedom from my "chosen destiny". I worked Friday nights till 9 p.m. and all day Saturday till 6 p.m. This seemed like a good idea for two reasons. I worked for clothing rather than money, since the income tax people would only want a piece of this extra income. But I would have new clothes for my main job.

Also the owner liked the idea as well, because he could have the whole weekend off. This would indeed work out great for all concerned and give me the freedom that I was looking for. These kids were just "excess baggage" that came along for the ride. Their mother was my soul interest.

I was to get yet another reality check from Amy because she decided I could buy her and the children clothing items as well. HOW SPECIAL IS THAT?!!!

Unfortunately for me the clothing store had items not only for children but women's/men's wear and even some sports items. It was like a small department store and Amy's eyes gleamed. There would be no shortage for her kids and herself from all my hours of work at this wonderful store.

I was now number three in the purchasing/pecking order of importance. Here again, I was to assist Amy with clothing costs for her and her children. Is this "special" or what? I was not only assisting to provide a roof over the little darling's heads; but now clothing for their very backs. BUT HEY . . . WASN'T THAT WHAT I HAD SIGNED UP FOR??

I was not the father, the provider for her children's needs; but somehow this duty was now laid on me. What a surprise!! I asked myself where their "natural" father was. Where was the clothing, the money, his taking the kids for the odd weekend? In fact wasn't he still responsible to provide the necessities of life or at least help out with them? If I had been thinking with my brain, instead of my penis, I would have known the answers to these questions. All of this should have been discussed with

Amy and I should have been thinking about this, in the course of our relationship. TOO LATE NOW YOU SUCKER!!!

There was no reason why I couldn't/shouldn't buy for Amy and her children. At least there was no logical and reasonable response. If I had made an issue of it, there would have been hell on the home-front. The little activity that I was enjoying would be cut off. Bringing clothing items home was always very beneficial to me, especially in the bedroom. We seemed to exchange sex for clothing, and the system seemed to work well.

Our lives had now totally changed; Amy and I were like strangers, except in the bedroom, and how I longed for my old lifestyle. In Amy's defence, she had been a good mother and that had to come first. But this was a new world to me, because I had been number one. The "bottom spot" was a long and unhappy fall; but one spot that I would surely have to get used to.

Whenever I "gave", then I was a person of worth. Otherwise I was just expected to remain at the bottom spot of importance, until once again the giving process returned. Boy, how had I been so stupid? How could I not see the parallels between these two elements of pleasure? I guess I was always to feel like a failure in life; but my goal to find that that special person and a happy lifestyle still eluded me. I carried on with this so-called happy family life and hoped there might be a change.

I was in my own little world of make believe, that there might be light at the end of the tunnel and that given time, good things always came to those who waited. Either I had to accept the lifestyle at hand or get my balls back; to have yet another breakaway. Amy had reached the golden ring of her desires for the moment; but another life-altering situation was coming into play. Amy had seen a new home construction speculation in her travels and now she laid this new idea on me, when I was in my weakened state of pleasure with her. She knew I would be more receptive at this time to her request because she could be very seductive and pleasing when a plan was in her head. A hot, sexual encounter would ensure her a better chance at getting her way. Amy told me that the home was larger, on a bigger lot, out in the country. What a great time we could have deciding all the exterior and interior details. Amy said *"Like you, I feel that our marriage has gotten stale, and by working together to choose all the finishes, it would bring us closer. How great would that be?"*

I FELL FOR THIS HOOK, LINE AND SINKER!! Again the kids were put in the background and I was again to be "number one". Amy and I spent a lot of time together picking out this and that for the new home. We often had to go to the dealer to find just the right item that she wanted. We would often go out for dinner on the weekends after seeing home items, and the time together was like the "old times". We were actually forming a tighter bond, or so I thought. The bedroom was always hot and heavy, with much pleasure . . . very memorable for both of us.

But as they say, all good things do eventually have to come to an end. As the final touches had been ironed out, all that remained to be done was the installation. I was again going to the bottom of the pile of importance, to await another call for my time or my money.

Amy's interest in me as well as our regular sexual encounters was more distant, since she had accomplished her mission of getting this new home for her and her children. I was just tagging along for the ride, and I was to have to adjust to this lifestyle but again be in the basement of importance. I had acquired all the items on Amy's wish list and my duty for the moment was done.

The land of milk, honey and happiness that I was so hopeful for was just a passing thought. I really did have to "either shit or get off the pot" as the saying goes. Did I have balls enough to break away from Amy or do I just be like a puppet, go along as if everything in my world was okay?

It wasn't long till I felt the feeling of a storm cloud heading my way, and that made me even more uncomfortable. Amy had always been very much in debt and had decided without my knowledge, to quit her job with the government and take her severance and pay off all her debts. When she finally told me of her decision to quit; it was too late as she had already done the deed. She told me she just wanted to lie around for the summer; take things easy; mellow out (God knows what she had to mellow out over) and then she would look for a job in the fall.

I heard bells, whistle, and saw red flashing lights all going off at the same time inside my head. I asked her how we were going to manage all the household expenses. She seemed not too excited and simply said she needed a change in her job and her lifestyle, so *"Suck it up big boy"*.

There seemed to be no point to trying to discuss the matter further. She was not interested in anything logical or reasonable, about why she shouldn't have quit or about our future expenses. This was the final straw for me; it had awakened my "real" brain, and I told Amy that this was **not** acceptable. Either she had to get another job right away or get the hell out!! I was going to stick to the statement I had made come hell or high water. Amy had long realized that she would be coming out of our marriage with a lot more than she actually put into it.

My parents loaned me the money to buy her out so that I could keep the home. I think this was the most heart-breaking day of my life, when I had to go to my parents to bail me out of this situation. When you are a child parents are always there to look after your best interests; but as an adult you should be long past this stage in life. You should be standing on your own two feet and looking after your own problems, not having to go to them to plead for money because of the situation you got yourself into. THIS WAS INDEED A VERY BLACK DAY IN MY LIFE!!

When I arrived home one day after work, I found the new home totally empty, and the car I had bought Amy was not there either. Should this have been a surprise? Not really!!! She still had the keys for the house and possession being nine-tenths of the law. She simply helped herself to everything. I had been helpful for the last time in Amy's needs, so I guess she thought my job of "looking after her" was finally finished!

My new home was totally empty, just like my life at the moment. What my future held for me was a total unknown, and I asked myself once again, *"What does the future hold for me?"* This thought entered my brain slowly and registered there.

A co-worker heard of my separation, and in a very hurtful way told me *"IT'S THE SCREWING YOU GET, FOR THE SCREWING YOU GOT IN MARRIAGE"*. This message just somehow kept repeating itself over and over in my brain. What a sad thought! If it weren't for

BAD luck, I'd have NO luck at all. This thought too, kept repeating inside my head.

I was totally shaken with this experience in my life, to the point that I withdrew to a "non-acknowledgement" of the opposite sex. I now was involved strictly with work, doing outside yard work around the home and basically just being "one with myself". The search for a soul-mate or to enter into another relationship, to even thinking about that, was long gone for now.

This existence would continue for many years, because I had convinced myself that I was not capable of a loving relationship; nor did I have the skills or the knowledge about how to go about finding my life's wish of happiness and finding my one true love, to have a life-partner till death do us part.

SO ENDS THE FIRST SEGMENT OF MY LIFE . . . A DISMAL FAILURE TO THE TEST OF A GOOD AND HAPPY LIFE!!!

I busied myself with small decorating home improvements, like simple painting and papering the walls in my home. I thought these simple changes would put my personal touch in my home, and erase any signs of anyone else living here. I also took an interest in gardening and even attempted to do some landscaping to the yard to change its outward appearance Again, I put my mark of ownership to this property.

I purchased trees and shrubs, when they were on sale at the nursery, to beautify the grounds. The railway tracks were within a quarter mile of my home. As fate would have it; they were replacing the old railway ties with new ones, so there would be a ready supply of railway ties to use in my landscape design. I would make nightly trips to the railway track site and load my trunk with two or three of the ties and then head back to my home to unload them. The sheer weight of the ties lowered the rear end of my car, to the point I was afraid to overload it, in case I did some permanent damage to the springs in the car. Consequently, many trips would be involved to get the quantity of ties that I was after. Several nights and many trips, I had "borrowed" enough railway ties to make a 16x12x3 foot high flower/shrub bed at the end of my driveway. I watched for specials at the local nursery and then began to plot out the landscape items that I wished to purchase. I actually had to pat myself on the back at the completion of the job, because it showcased a very decorative, colourful, and well thought out garden display. I had just enough railway ties left to make two small railway-tie beds approximately 4x4 in my front yard for additional landscape appeal. In the two beds, I planted three white birch trees and put white stones at the base for an added effect. I was again pleased with the end results, because my front yard was now taking on a little personality and it added to the curb-side appeal to those driving by the property.

I was becoming quite pleased with my efforts, and the best part was that even though I was alone and lost to the outside world, I was putting my time to good use, and not missing feminine companionship. As my finances started to improve a 14x32 redwood cedar wood deck was added to the rear of the home. I also put in a 14x16 paved stone area at the end of the deck, accompanied by a cedar bench for sitting. I also built a small flower bed attached to this paved stone area where I planted four small trees for beautification.

My neighbour even commented at how well my landscaping was progressing. He even stated that he had six small maple trees that I could have for free, as they would look good at the end of my yard. I was now entering the conclusion of my ideas and space to plant anymore items. It was about now, that time was starting to weigh heavily on my mind; so another project to attempt was the order of the day.

The project that came to mind was to fence in my backyard as this would be a big undertaking and eat into a lot of my free time which was the whole idea anyway. My lot was 100x200 and to enclose this space would be very costly. I would have to come up with some way of being able to accomplish it. I was talking with a friend who knew of an old barn structure that could provide the boards needed for the fence, so why didn't I approach the owner and see if a price deal could be worked out for the barn-boards. In fact I did contact the owner and he said I could have all the barn boards I wanted for free, but two conditions applied.

The first condition was that I had to totally take down the entire structure for free and secondly that I did not come after him if I hurt myself in the process. This was a fantastic deal for me and I quickly agreed to the terms. This would be a two-fold win for me, as I would get all the wood for free, and the process would definitely eat into a lot of my free time, and my mind could remain blank.

I busied myself with this task at hand and soon discovered that it was indeed a major undertaking. This whole new plan of mine would take a lot of time to complete, but what would I be doing otherwise with my time, but to be aware that I was alone. Then I would start to feel sorry for myself.

Several months and many trips later from the barn site to my home, and the work was getting done. The barn board pile was getting bigger and becoming a topic of conversation with the neighbours. They were curious about what I was going to build with the material. At the final completion of the barn dismantling, I seriously looked at the mammoth barn-board pile, and thought that I had enough wood to build a small house, let alone a wooden fence.

I was now going into the next phase of the building the fence enclosure for my back yard. My neighbour had a post-hole digger, and I was to discover the hardest part of the fence building project. Manually digging post holes was playing havoc with my soft hands and blisters on blisters would appear. My hands would literally ache after each day of digging holes. After several weeks of digging and the approval of all my neighbours that indeed it had passed inspection, I was ready to go into the next phase.

I ordered posts to install into the holes I had dug, and also 2x4's wood framing to be attached to the posts. I also ordered the cement to secure the post themselves into the ground. I was now about to learn the art of cement mixing, or should I say the proper method of mixing cement to the correct consistency to do its job of holding up the weight of the fence.

My old neighbour, who in his day was a jack of all trades, took me under his wing and proceeded to teach me. Once I had learned the technique, I was off to apply my new skills to the actual job at hand. Here again, after the last post was set into place, I took pride in myself that the fence was starting to take shape.

After a couple of days to let the cement totally cure, I was ready to attach the 2x4's to the post structure. A few more days later and that job too had been completed, and now the actual pile of barn boards would come into play. The mammoth job of attaching the barn boards to the fencing structure was at hand. This job was a slow process as the boards were attached manually with hammer and nails. A "nail gun" was not even thought of and nobody even new of its existence. This was even before the concept was thought of, because this was in the early 1970's. Several weeks later, this job was completed. As I looked from my deck into the back yard at my handiwork, it was very satisfying to see that all my labour skills and the knowledge that I had been given had totally materialized into a finished project. As I sat there being so "full of myself", I looked to my right and discovered that still the pile of barn boards seemed not to have totally dwindled. What was I to do with all that remained?

Why not build a shed? I had never built one; I had lots of wood, and definitely lots of time on my hands. So that concept became the next challenge. Once again I called upon my old neighbour for his opinion and skills to enter into this project. My old neighbour, Walter, described the materials and method of shed construction to me. I realized that Walter would again have to teach me additional skills to complete such a structure.

The first stage was to lay a cement floor structure and lucky for me, Walter had a cement mixer. DUH!! Why hadn't he told me before? I had hand mixed all the post-hole cement filler but as Walter told me *"Too big a quantity of cement all at one time for use"* and that did make sense.

Walter was just like having my own personal supervisor as he instructed on the size and depth of the soil to be removed. At least as I was working, there was company and a man with a keen eye for every detail in the total scheme of the project. Once this process got the "OK" from Walter, it was time for me to bring over the cement mixer. Here again, Walter was very informative, an excellent teacher, and one who had patience with this new student.

Time had to pass as Walter said *"We have to let the cement set and cure"*, before the next phase could begin. A couple of days later Walter was over and said to me *"Time to get busy, as time is a-wasting"*. We entered the wood framing process, followed by the barn-boards being attached and the shed was now starting to take shape. All that remained to be done now was to put on a wood decking and to shingle the roof. Walter's skills and knowledge was invaluable to me as the whole process would not have been completed without all his talents. I wanted to pay Walter for his time and skills in all the projects that he had assisted me with. But he would not hear of it, and just headed home. I spoke to his wife Edna and told her that Walter would not take any money for all he had done for me. She said that I could purchase a new garden hose for him if I really insisted on giving him a present.

Edna said *"I have not seen him so happy in a long time, to have someone who needed his time and talents was the greatest gift of all and that the garden hose was not really necessary."* But she was sure he would appreciate having a new hose. I bought him a power washer and was thrilled to do so, as it was a small payment for all he had done for me.

When I presented it to Walter he just beamed ear to ear, and I knew that I had indeed made this man happy with his new toy. There were many attachments and things that he could wash down with this power washer.

Time was still ticking onward but now seemed to move so slowly. I had run out of work projects, and now the boredom was back in my life. As fate would have it, another neighbour was moving into a retirement home and wasn't going to be allowed to take his dog with him. Learning of the dog's fate, Walter came over and said *"Why don't you take it? You now have the yard for it"?* It seemed like a perfect solution for both the dog and me, a home for the dog, and I would have a constant live-in friend for myself.

This is how Willie entered my life, and made me a happy man. It was great to have a best friend, a companion for walks, and someone to talk to during the lonely nights. It was also nice to have a friend greet me when I came home from work, rather than just the four walls closing in on me. I received much love and affection from my time spent with Willie. Now life seemed to have a purpose.

For the first time in a long time, I was no longer alone, and my world seemed happier place. But once again, fate was to raise its head in my direction. I had stopped for gas on my way home after work. Who do you think was there? Erin had also stopped to fill up before going home. What would be the chances of this meeting ever happening? Both of us did a double-take and the polite thing to do was to speak. We had a light conversation with one another.

This seemed both pleasurable and yet brief, so we decided to go to the Tim Horton's on the corner and really get caught up on one another's life and all the years in between. What had happened to whom, the people we knew in general, family issues, health issues of both our parents? Time just slowly drifted on, until having supper together seemed the right way to end our chance encounter.

I had been transformed in that brief time frame to once again wanting to date Erin. The time we had just spent together felt somehow comfortable. It was like putting on an old sweater; it just seemed to make you feel good. The comfort zone you had been seeking was realized. Erin and I had talked over a multitude of issues like . . . our time together, the reasons why we had drifted apart, that we had not found someone in years to settle down with, and that time <u>was</u> marching on. We both thought it might be time again to explore a relationship with one another. Had it not been fate that had brought us together in this chance encounter in the first place?

We both had aged and hopefully learned from our mistakes, and we did at one point in our lives have a connection to one another. Consequently, we decided to give it another go. The next weekend we had planned to go out for dinner and to a show. I told Erin that I would call her midweek to finalize plans and to confirm it was still set for that weekend. I did talk with Erin midweek as promised and our plans were confirmed and the time set for our get-together.

When I arrived to pick her up, I was greeted at the doorway by Rebecca. I was sort of taken aback, as I was expecting Erin to open the door. She and I stood there motionless for a moment, staring at each other, a state of shock on both our faces. Apparently neither of us had been prepared for that moment. Rebecca broke the ice and said *"Hello stranger, nice to see you again, come on in"*.

Rebecca told me that Erin was still upstairs getting ready, to have a seat and she would get me a drink. It seemed like an hour for these few moments to pass. Small talk between us seemed difficult; but we both struggled to carry on a conversation. I'm not sure if Rebecca was thinking about our loving sessions of along ago; but they were sure dancing in **my** head. They were bringing back pleasant memories we embraced while Erin was asleep in the next bedroom.

These thoughts, the very moment of being together again all added to a difficult conversation between us. Then the phone rang, and I thought to myself, AH! Saved by the Bell!

As Rebecca was talking on the phone, Erin came down the stairway and said *"Glad Rebecca got you a drink. Sorry I took so long in getting ready"*. Being the perfect gentleman, I said *"Not a problem"*. But in my mind I was thinking "thank God it didn't take any longer as I was feeling quite uncomfortable spending time with Rebecca".

We went out to dinner and to a show, and even drinks following the conclusion of the evening. I actually had a very enjoyable evening with Erin and she had said that it was a great evening as well. She kissed me good night at the doorway and I was both surprised and pleased, as we said our good nights, the "call you soon", and I headed for home.

On my drive home I thought why had this date seemed so enjoyable? Was it just because it was the two of us and not the usual group? Was it now because we were older, we realized that we wanted a connection to one another, and that fate had indeed put us back together? I could come to no conclusion, so I put all those thoughts to the back of my brain, turned up the music on the radio and concentrated on the task of driving home safely.

Erin and I again dated on the weekend, and I was even surprised when she asked me to her family's home for Sunday lunch. Her parents greeted me like a long lost son, and truly made me feel at home. I think at this point in our renewed relationship, I was both confused and thrilled as everything seemed so perfect. This was the relationship that I had wanted so many years ago, to feel connect to Erin and to her family. Was this now a dream, or was it truly happening? Pinch me and awaken me was the thought that bounced through my head. But I did truly feel happy once again, and hoped that the bubble (if there was one) did not break any time soon.

However, there was a bubble to break in our future. After just a few weeks of dating, Erin slowly started to bring back the familiar group, to go along with us on our supposed "couple's" night out. She had reverted back to her old ways of doing things with the group and forgetting to include me in her plans. There were weekends away with Rebecca and even planned holidays away together. Again, there were the large house parties, which I was included in, but somehow the connection that I thought was a strong bond this second time around, was just like the shifting of grains of sand, ever so gently moving in different directions. All these outside forces seemed to control it.

This is how my mind and my heart were feeling . . . like a fish caught. I was being played by the fisherman. Erin had set the hook and I had taken the bait . . . LOCK, STOCK and BARREL. She was taking her sweet time, enjoying the moment before she wanted to reel me in. Erin liked having everything her way. I was the sucker fish and I let her do this to me, yet again. Why? I had reverted back to this spineless creature, having no backbone. What was the attraction? What was the hold? What was I doing to myself? Was I so desperate for someone in my life, that I would again accept any and all of Erin's old ways?

Apparently I had hit the nail on the head with this statement. I went along for the long, miserable, uncertainty of a future that lay before me. What would it take to get me to come to my senses? Surprise! Rebecca again came back into my life, filling the empty void left by Erin, who left me feeling unwanted and not needed.

The old routine of cleaning up after the house parties, seemed like my job, or so I thought it was. Rebecca was knocking on the wall between our mutual bedrooms; Erin was drunk and sleeping in another bedroom, and life seemed like before. It was like I had never left this existence . . . as though time had been frozen.

It had been a long dry spell since I had last enjoyed the pleasures of sexual activity, and Rebecca wanted to please. Who was I not to accept? I rose from my bed to go and enjoy the pleasures of two bodies uniting as one; to feel the ecstasy and the fireworks once again going off throughout my body. Then I would return to my bedroom and wait for morning as Erin would rise to start another day, and was none the wiser. I had to quickly erase the glow from my face before this occurred.

This lifestyle again settled in as a normal routine, and wondered if I should be the one to start rocking the boat. I was having great sex with Rebecca; Erin was still somewhat involved in my life, and best of all I had something to look forward to some weekends.

Therefore I accepted this connection to Erin and her rules, and her lifestyle. I really had nothing better in my life at the moment. As the saying goes . . . "SOMETHING IS MUCH BETTER THAN NOTHING". So I went along for the ride and whatever time limit that was to be involved, would be my fate.

I was starting to acquire a desire, a feeling of wanting more activity, wanting to be more connected to people throughout the week, not just on weekends. I was reading the newspaper one day and had discovered an ad to join a newly formed bowling league. I decided I would look into this venture. I had grown up in St. Thomas, so there was sure to be a lot of people that I would know, and it could be a night out through the week. This would help break up my week before the upcoming weekend; so it seemed that this could be the perfect solution.

Willie seemed conscious of the fact that yet another night that I would be leaving him alone; but this time it would only be for a couple of hours. I didn't hang on to the guilt feeling that I was experiencing. Willie was a good friend, and seemed to take this in his stride, as he always greeted me with his warm, tail-wagging welcome home. Willie would soon know my routine as well as I did myself, and I would still be spending a lot of time with him. Everything was going to be alright in his world.

When the first sign-up night of bowling came, I was my usual self . . . the last person to arrive and predominately the bulk of the teams were already made up. I just made it in the nick of time and I was the last person they needed, as the bowling league was now full. The league had now decided on a Monday night schedule as their league night, and I was so hoping it would have been near the end of the week.

There went my idea of breaking up my week; but I had signed up, so what the heck. I would go with the flow. The following Monday night was the official start of the season and so "LET THE GAMES BEGIN" resounded in my head as the first few balls started rolling down the alleys. There were 6 people to a team and 16 teams. My determination to have fun was set in motion. As the weeks rolled by, everyone was breaking the ice with one another and I did indeed know several people in the league; but there were a lot I didn't know. On the team that I had been assigned to, I didn't know a single person; but they all seemed a friendly lot, and good times and laughter flowed.

I was pleased that I had joined up as there were couples and singles on all the different teams we played. So it was always different people you would meet each week. It was not long and everyone was getting to know one other, and a fun bowling league had been established.

For one couple on my team, the husband was seldom there, so we were always looking for a spare bowler for our team, or we just played with a 5 member team handicap. The lady's name was Anne Marie, and soon she and I were enjoying conversations with one another. One bowling night after the games were done, she asked if I wanted to join her and other members of different teams to go for a coffee. Of course I accepted. Anne Marie and I soon became aware that it was now just us left at the table. Everyone else had finished their beverage and had gone. I cracked a joke and said *"Do you think it was something I said that drove them away"*?

We both had a good laugh over it, and I said to Anne Marie that I had better walk her to her car, as it was very dark behind the bowling alley where she had parked. She was happy with my offer and quickly agreed. We made small talk as we walked to where her car was parked. This only took a few minutes and we arrived at the vehicle.

I guess I had been lost in the conversation, whatever the reason, but I was enjoying this time with her, and I was sorry to see it end. I had just said good night to her, and was turning to leave. Anne Marie grabbed my arm, and turned me back towards her, and her lips were embracing mine. We entered into a full blown passionate kiss, our arms entwined around each other, and we were lost to each other's passion. We got into the car, struggling to remove clothing, all the while kissing, touching and caressing each other's body. The desire to be connected was strong.

We wanted that intimate moment of pleasure, of giving to one another, of having all the bells and whistles of the excitement of full connection. We were still fighting for a comfortable spot to unite in the back seat of the car. And you know that where there is a will, there is a way!

The hour was getting late; I told her we had better leave before a cop showed up, or worse her husband came looking for her. Anne Marie said *"Maybe a cop, but never my husband, because we are talking divorce"*. The mystery of where the husband had been on bowling night had just been solved. But Anne Marie said *"Yes, you are right, we had better leave"*, and with that we struggled to get our clothing on, one last kiss, and each of us departed for our homes.

On my drive home I kept asking myself, *"What had just happened? Was it a dream? Was I losing it"*? I looked at my watch for reassurance, because I was driving and realized the hour, and then said to myself *"I just had pleasure with a stranger. What was I doing"*? Another married woman! At this stage, she was still married, but a pending divorce was in her future. Were there children? What the hell was I thinking about? It surely was a one night fling, and I wasn't really going to get caught up in this kind of affair again; or was I?

Willie greeted me on my return, and even seemed to have a puzzled look on his face at least it seemed to be. I was later than normal, for his nightly walk and his treats. His total schedule had been altered. In his own way, Willie showed me his displeasure, and that he was not impressed one little bit. He took great delight in a multitude of stops, sniffing here and there, not wanting to walk fast. In general, Willie wanted me to know he was not happy with me, so I had better clean up my act, and get back to the normal schedule.

The following Monday bowling night was at hand, and there was an open spot and Anne Marie was smiling widely! I don't know if it was just me but it felt like everyone was staring at us, and I felt uncomfortable. I quickly realized that I was just having a guilty conscience for my past week of pleasure with this lady, and that all was normal. I just had to get a grip on myself, and get into the evening of bowling. Anne Marie was wearing a sweater with a horse image on its front, complete with string to create the effect of a horse's tail. I decided to break the ice with the group and the unsettling feeling that I was having, so I opened my big mouth. I said to Anne Marie *"Nice piece of tail!"*, before I totally realized what I had just said.

Everyone broke into laughter, which surprisingly seemed to ease my tension, and the bowling began. After we were finished, Anne Marie spoke into my ear and said *"Walk me to my car again please"*. I was eager to comply with her request and so we headed in the direction of her car.

We were having small talk along the way, and she told me that she had plenty of time tonight, as her husband had left town to go for a week long business meeting in Toronto. She further added that he wouldn't be home till late Sunday night. Anne Marie then said *"If you want that piece of tail, you were talking about earlier, lets head for your place"*. I just smiled pleasantly and off we went in the direction of my home in Talbotville.

It took approximately 15 minutes to arrive at my home, and all the while my excitement was mounting. Anne Marie had never been to my home before and as she got out of her car, she said *"I thought we were never going to get to your home; it's further than I thought"*.

Once inside I offered Anne Marie a glass of wine and asked if she would like to see my two-storey home. She said that indeed she would like the full tour, so we began. We took our drinks and started to go from room to room on each floor until we finally reached my bedroom.

Anne Marie then said *"This is the room I have been looking for"*, as she grabbed me in her arms.

A passionate kiss was followed by the slow removal of our clothing. Being the perfect gentleman, I was assisting her to speed up the process. The moment of lust had now peaked, and we were as one, lost in a moment of pleasure, that sent the thermostat reading of satisfaction to its very peak. I could not believe the excitement, the pleasure and the total satisfaction that I had experienced, as I laid there in a pool of my own sweat.

I told Anne Marie with both my actions and my words how fantastic this moment had been and she just smiled and said *"It has been a long while for me as well, to have such an enjoyable sexual partner, because my husband has no desire for my body"*. I thought to myself, this guy must be nuts! How could he not want this pleasure? I asked Anne Marie that very question, and she stated *"He is either tired of sex with me, or I think/I know he has another woman who pleases him now"*.

I pulled her close to me, gentle kisses to her body, rolling my hands over her body, and soon the pleasure meter was ticking again, and we were making love. When we again laid there in a pool of sweat, Anne Marie glanced at the clock and said *"Oh my Lord, look at the time."* As she scrambled to get her clothes on, and trying to stop me from wanting to take them off again, she said *"I really have to be heading for home"*. I walked her to her car with just my housecoat on, gave her a final kiss good night, and she was off down the road. I thought to myself, as I headed indoors, how wonderful joining that bowling league had been. It was far beyond my wildest expectations. A happy sex life seemed to be presenting itself and my well of sexual pleasure was not going to remain dry in the forthcoming future.

I was both surprised and shocked on Tuesday after my supper was done to receive a phone call from Anne Marie. She wanted to know about my day and what was I up to at the moment. Could she come out and see me? The immediate answer that came from my mouth was *"looking forward to seeing you"* as I hung up the phone. I thought to myself, how nice to be on the receiving end of a phone call rather than being the one having to make the call. It had been my experience when I called Erin, I was always hoping she would pick up or at least return my phone calls.

Anne Marie soon arrived and I surprised her with both a kiss of welcome and a glass of wine. She exclaimed that was the nicest "welcome home" greeting she had received in a very long time. We sat on the couch watching the television, and were cuddled up on the couch, just enjoying the time and the closeness to one another.

We had both just finished our wine, and as I got up to refresh our drinks, she pulled me back and greeted me with a passionate kiss. We both simultaneously placed our glasses on the table and became like teenagers, rolling on top of one another, tugging, pulling, and kissing each other's bodies. Anne Marie said *"let's go to bed, where we can be more comfortable"*, and we rose from the couch and moved in the direction of the stairway. I thought this was a good plan, to let her make the decision to go to bed rather than me. It would look like I wanted to be with her, to have that special time alone, enjoying the closeness to each another, and not just looking for that sexual encounter.

This was indeed the plan of action that I had attempted to put into place, as I felt that *slowly and surely* was the way to go for the rewards that I was seeking. We had just entered the bedroom and a transformation instantly occurred. Since we had been quiet and sedate on the walk upstairs, once through the bedroom doorway, we instantly started pulling at each other's clothing. I was anxious to have my hands on her soft, full, breasts yet again and to run my hands over all the crevices of her body and to have her to do the same to my body.

This total stimulation of both our bodies . . . internal and external . . . was heightening the ecstasy for the union of our two bodies, as we headed for the bed and the pleasures that lay ahead. We were both transformed, our bodies were struggling to reach that ecstasy, the point of our pleasure meter peaking, both seeking the fulfillment of the union with one another. The explosion within both our bodies and minds as we coupled was soon at hand.

We were now laying there in our own pools of sweat, each of us holding one another, slowly caressing each other as we beamed, showing the total sexual satisfaction of our encounter that we had and were still enjoying.

I thought that the night was still young, and possibly both our sexual meters may be stimulated again, before the night was over and another round of excitement may occur. I did not have to wait long as Anne Marie said *"Well big boy, will one round be enough for you"?*

I just smiled back at her and she instantly knew that I was hoping we would stay here in bed and round two was a definite in my mind. She said again *"I was hopeful as well, as I want to taste another round of pleasure to bring my evening of desire to a full conclusion".* We made small talk about each other's day, and the upcoming week's activities we would be involved in. My hands started to roam over her body in a slow process which was doing the trick of getting us both in the mood and our horny meters were rising. It was not long, no pun intended, before the desire to partake in the enjoyment of each other's bodies was at hand.

The moment of lust had again peaked, and soon our bodies were as one, lost in the moment of complete pleasure that indeed set off the bells, whistles and fireworks inside our heads. I could not believe the total experience of pleasure and satisfaction that I had just experienced, as I laid there exhausted again, in my own pool of sweat. My heart was beating like an Indian war drum, and my energy was totally gone. All that remained was a limp body.

Anne Marie was also laying there breathing heavily, all the while smiling. Finally she said *"That was fantastic, I could really get to enjoy this nightly; but I do not know if you would be up to it, because having sex may become less interesting to you on a regular basis"?* I just smiled back at her and said *"Honey I enjoy making love, and I will never tire of it, and with you as my partner in bed, the likelihood of that happening seems very remote".*

This statement seemed both to please her and also to set her mind at ease. I think she thought herself too pushy, for asking to come out to see me. As it turned out for me, this had been the perfect response, the one she had been hoping for. Anne Marie again looked at the clock and exclaimed that the hour was late and that she had to go as her baby sister was watching her children and she too would need to be getting home.

Again being the perfect gentleman, and wearing only my housecoat, I walked her to her car and kissed her goodnight. She said she would call tomorrow, and off down the road she went.

In fact, she did call on Wednesday, and asked *"Do you remember our conversation of last night; or did the great sex erase all those thoughts?"* I had to admit to her that everything she had said did not totally register, as my hands and mind were on her body and on my enjoyment. Perhaps some of the words that she said **may** have been lost. Again, this was the perfect answer because it let me off the hook about recalling the total conversation. It also pleased Anne Marie to know that I was totally enjoying her body.

She said *"Do you remember that I said I couldn't come out till Friday night"?* I had to reply that I had not remembered that comment and she just laughed aloud. Fortunately for me she liked my answer, and she said *"It will give you time to build up your strength, as it will be in the bedroom we will be spending our weekend"*. At this statement my brain was doing a dance in my head about the forthcoming weekend of pleasure that lay ahead for me. I replied *"I will miss you"* and she responded with *"I hope you do miss me and not just the sex"*!

It was only going to be really two days without sex since Friday would only be day three and the pleasure meter would be on full charge. I said out loud *"Look out Anne Marie. A marathon of sex is about to come your way."* I was developing a ravenous desire for daily sex and this woman seemed more than a willing partner in this venture. She also had been on a long dry spell of having no sex, and her well of pleasure also needed to be filled to the brim.

Friday. It seemed that the whole day just dragged. The expectations constantly danced in my head, and so I was totally unprepared for the phone call I was about to receive. Out of the clear blue Erin had decided to call, and as we were making some small talk, she actually apologized for not calling in quite awhile. She said she was also sorry for not returning any of my phone messages; but she had noticed that I had not called her all week.

"OH MY GOODNESS!!!" flashed through my head. But I said nothing in response. I simply replied *"I knew you must have been very busy, or you would have taken time to call"*. WHAT A CROCK OF YOU KNOW WHAT!!

This seemed to momentarily be the right answer for Erin, and so our conversation continued. Otherwise with her quick temper, she would have hung up the phone. In hindsight, maybe I should have said *"You seldom call, so I just gave up calling you"*, because then I wouldn't have to come up with a good reason why I was busy this weekend.

I was not prepared to give up my whole weekend of sex with Anne Marie, on the off chance that I could have sex with Rebecca. None of this would be forthcoming from Erin. I told Erin that it was nice to hear from her but that I was sorry we hadn't talked to each other through the week. My company knew that I was single and my time was quite flexible. Consequently, they were sending me out of town on business this weekend.

"I had already agreed to go since I didn't know of any plans with you for this upcoming weekend." This had occurred numerous times before, going out of town on company business, throughout our relationship; so it was a very creditable statement. It also made sure that I was unavailable to see her this weekend.

Erin said *"I'm truly sorry I didn't call earlier this week, as we could have had some time together and you wouldn't have had to work all weekend. Please call me when you get home Sunday night and we can make plans for the next weekend together."* I thought to myself if Erin only knew the wonderful work I was going to do this weekend she would probably take great delight in shooting me. Instead, what I did say was *"I'm sorry as well that I will not be available to spend time with you. I will look forward to seeing and speaking with you soon".*

As I hung up the phone I realized what a smart boy I had been. There would be no surprise visits from Erin because she knew I would not be at home. That would relieve any pressure of her sudden appearance off my mind, and the only pressure I had to be concerned with came from down below.

I got a phone call from Anne Marie just after I had finished my supper. She said *"I am sorry that I haven't called earlier. Would you like to have a guest for the whole weekend?"* I knew we would be seeing a lot of each other over the weekend, but I did not realize she was actually going to literally be staying all weekend with me. I couldn't readily reply as my thoughts where going a mile a minute; but I finally was able to say *"How wonderful! Do I understand correctly you will be spending the whole weekend with me"?* Anne Marie said *"When there was a moment of silence, I thought you might not be interested; but, when I heard your reply, I was very happy knowing you were very excited about my proposal".*

She told me further, that her parents were taking her sons. This was the first time I knew that her children were both boys. I knew of their existence, but not that they were "boys". Her parents were taking them away for a fun-filled weekend, and she would otherwise be all alone. That was why she could spend the whole weekend.

She also told me that her parents knew that the boys were confused and upset with their parent's relationship and the pending divorce, so a change in their daily routine was hopefully going to smooth things out a little. She said *"It might be a little later before I am able to come out, but I am coming as soon as my parents take the kids"*. She arrived around eight o'clock and said *"It seems strange moving in for the weekend with you and not having the boys around"*.

As she came in, I quickly gave her a kiss, a warm hug, and said *"I'm so happy you are here, and not having to share you with anyone all weekend"*. I got us a glass of wine and put her small suitcase in the hallway, and we headed for the couch in the family room. This time seemed different as we just sat there, making small talk with another, occasionally glancing at the television and I thought "how like an old married couple we seemed". We were not emotionally involved on the couch as before, but instead we seemed very calm, cool, and collected. I brought up this point a little later in the evening and Anne Marie just said *"I'm sorry, I was just thinking about my boys and how I would not see them all weekend"*. Then she said *"Maybe I should not have come to your home"*. I quickly said *"Nonsense, you're just being a good mother with natural feelings and I am still very happy to have you here with me and to be close to you"*.

Again this seemed like the appropriate response, as she leaned over and placed a passionate kiss on my lips and said *"Take me to bed. Make passionate love to me. Hold me and never let me go"*. I was more than ready to comply. In fact I had been excited, and waiting for this moment all day. I couldn't believe my ears as I said *"Your request is my command. I shall take you to the stars and beyond"*.

We headed upstairs and in our desire to be together, left her suitcase in the downstairs hallway. We had hardly entered the bedroom and she was upon me . . . pushing me to the bed, holding me down and kissing and fondling me. In fact, she was driving me totally crazy with excitement.

I told her I wanted her, needed her and I even said *"I love you"*. I suddenly realized what I said and hoped she hadn't heard that comment. Now I was allowed to begin to pull her clothing off and to begin to totally excite her and drive her crazy for that special connection we both wanted.

We both wanted our pleasure meters to be totally satisfied . . . minds and bodies at the height of ecstasy. Shortly afterwards as we lay quietly beside each other, Anne Marie said *"My God, you are so horny! It's only been two days. What would you be like in a week without sex?"* We both just laughed and cuddled in each other's arms . . . totally satisfied. Soon sleep overtook us.

As we woke in late morning, I said, *"How about starting the day with a bang?"* Anne Marie replied *"If you're up to it; so am I. But I cannot believe your sex drive!"* Once again, we made love, but this time very slowly and very passionately. There was a bond of tightness forming between us. I was not sure at this moment; but thought I might actually be falling in love with this woman. Maybe I was just fooling myself. Maybe it was just the lusty sex talking.

While Anne Marie was having her shower, I quickly took Willie for his walk and then put him in the backyard to finish burning off his energy. I got him breakfast and then came inside, surprised to see Anne Marie wearing my housecoat and cooking breakfast.

"I hope you don't mind. I couldn't find my suitcase till I came downstairs." I said *"It looks better on you than on me. Besides it makes for less clothing I have to take off your body after breakfast."* She replied *"You are kidding, right?"* I said *"I think of us as a newly-wed couple and I plan to make love to you all weekend! So you better eat hardy so you have your strength for the upcoming events."*

"My God; you are serious! I will definitely be sore by the end of the weekend" she said. Neither of us was fully dressed most of the weekend. At the drop of a hat, we were going to bed, to that zone of lusty pleasure. I knew that by the end of these few days that both our wells of sexual desires would indeed be filled. After all this was the challenge of the weekend was it not?

As in all good things, they eventually have to come to an end, or so it seems to be the case. After our Sunday morning session of making love and a quick breakfast, Anne Marie was to leave. She said *"I have laundry to do; housework and preparation for the kids' return. I want to spend time with my parents. My husband will also be returning, not that I am looking forward to that".* She said *"I hope you enjoyed our time and making love as much as I have. I find it very difficult to leave you now and hope you feel the same."* Being a gentleman, I walked Anne Marie to her car, in my housecoat, gave her a final kiss, a wave goodbye, and she was off down the road.

I thought, what a great weekend of pleasure I had definitely enjoyed, and I could hopefully look forward to this kind of weekend of total ecstasy, very soon again. But for the moment, I would just have to go with the flow, and see when the opportunity would again present itself.

In fact, as fate with all its outside forces totally in place, would see to this was only a one time event. Anne Marie's life would have much going on. People, work and life's situations would keep popping up. There would be no confirmation of a weekend of pleasure for the two of us in the near future.

I really had no plan for the rest of the day, so I thought I would take a nap, followed by a shower, and then a walk with Willie. My day would be complete. I didn't have to call Erin till later that night, so I might just as well enjoy the memories of the sexual delight of the weekend, and totally take in all its moments of pleasure that I received.

Willie was a little unhappy with me again, and paced around the room. He was not happy about the little time that we had been together this weekend. He was not his usual bubbly self; he was more laid-back, his head was low, and his eyes looked very sad. They say when you look into animals eyes that you are looking into the window of their soul.

I instantly realized how sad Willie was, and how ashamed of myself I was about the lack of time I had spent with him. I knew both in my mind and in my heart, that I had not been kind to my best friend and that I would have to work hard to bring the gleam back into his eyes, and to see his happiness wagging with pleasure.

I knew instantly that a change in my plans was needed. So the nap was put on hold, and I knew the balance of the day was indeed Willie's. I needed to win back his good graces and gain his forgiveness. Willie's attitude quickly changed as we played in the backyard. I was amazed how quickly he was forgiving me and didn't seem to be holding a grudge. We played the balance of the day. I would like to think that once Willie realized that he was special in my life again and that his world had been turned right side up again.

I even took him for a car ride to Port Stanley where we played fetch on the beach. He even went into the lake for a swim, although this going into the water did not make me too happy. I knew he would be full of sand, and my car would look like a sand box by the time we got home. I couldn't get mad because I had already been in his bad books over the weekend. After all, it was just sand. It would clean up with a little elbow grease and effort on my part.

When Willie and I arrived home, I towelled him off a little more and then brushed him thoroughly. He loved me brushing and combing his long hair, and I hope/imagined that I saw the gleam come back into his eyes. I was also happy with the time I had spent with Willie, and knew that I had chosen the right course for this day.

Coincidently we had both just finished our suppers at the same time and I took my place on the floor beside him in the family room. Willie was enjoying me stroking his head, my small kisses of affection to his body. With an almost human-looking smile on his face, he drifted off to dream world. Willie was content, happy and at peace, knowing we would be bonding for the rest of the evening. I was also enjoying this time with him, as I recalled how he had entered my world, and what a big impact he had made in my lonely life.

Willie was my friend, my companion, and roommate, which filled that void in my terrible life. I was thinking I had not been a good friend to him this weekend because my sexual pleasure had over-ridden my time with Willie. I promised myself and Willie that it would never happen again. Willie was of worth to me and I had not treated him as such, and that selfishness made me sad!

The phone suddenly rang, and it was Erin. *"Why did you not call me like you promised?"* It was the usual tone that I had become accustomed to from Erin. There was no friendly conversation first about how my weekend had gone. Was it all work and no play? Where did I go out of town?

Erin just got straight to the point of her business. She felt she had been offended, and therefore the reason for her tone of her voice. I told her that I had gone to the neighbours where Willie had been staying all weekend, and that we had gone for a longer than usual walk together, and had just gotten in. This seemed to pacify her for the moment as her tone slowly reverted to a gentler tone. Even the hostility was now gone.

We made small talk about the weekend, and I was sure to keep the questions about her and her weekend to avoid questions about mine. She liked to be the centre of attention, so that everything was good in her world. Because I knew her, then my world was also at peace. I even told her, with my fingers crossed, how I had missed her and the chance of being together.

This seemed to have done the trick because now she was sweet as pie. Erin told me about the great weekend party that she and Rebecca had put on, and now that she had talked with me, she was tired and going to bed. Erin said *"Be sure you call me through the week for our weekend plans"*, and as quickly the phone call had started, it was over. I guess Erin really did not have much to talk about as usual. Why did I expect anything more?

The very first thought that went through my head was that it just a "duty call" to see if I was at home. There seemed no genuine questions about love, concern or missing me, even a little.

Secondly I thought, well there was a party that I did not have to clean up after. Thirdly I thought about how vague her interest in our upcoming weekend plans seemed to really be. It was like, "give me a call, and if I am not busy, I can maybe squeeze you in". All these statements kept going over and over in my head. It was as if nothing in the conversation was of much importance. The total time on the phone with Erin left me feeling very sad. In my bubble world, I thought that talking with your lady of choice, was supposed to leave you happy. MY MISTAKE!

I took Willie for his last walk of the evening, all the while these three statements of Erin's kept running through my brain. As I returned home with Willie, I just said *"Come on boy, I'm tired; let's go to bed"*. My mind would not turn off and it left me with an empty, unsatisfied, feeling of rejection.

Although this had not really been the case, the feelings running through my mind made it seem so. I thought how could a great weekend of pleasure turn so quickly to this depressed feeling, after just one short talk with Erin?

Again, I thought about what I was doing to myself. Why was I giving Erin all this power? What was I thinking, or not thinking through? Why was I so weak when it came to Erin and how she treated me? It was a long sleepless night and I kept disturbing Willie with my flipping around in bed. I'm sure he did not enjoy a solid night of sleep either.

Monday morning I arose from bed, still tired and Willie slowly left the bed as well. We both headed downstairs, him for a drink of water and me to make my morning coffee.

I saw Anne Marie that evening at bowling; but she looked tired, sad and even acted distant toward me. Everyone on our bowling team asked her if she was feeling alright. She said *"My one son was ill through the night and I didn't get much sleep at all."* This seemed to answer everyone's curiosity about her condition and so we all continued with bowling. I thought to myself, as I heard others ask about Anne Marie's condition, that it was not my imagination at play. It was an honest reply to their question.

Anne Marie said in my ear *"Walk me to my car after bowling is done please."* I just smiled in response. As we were walking to the cars, she said *"I had a terrible fight with my husband last night when he arrived home. He packed up some of his things and has gone . . . this time for good".* She also told me that boys had heard everything, and they too were very upset.

She said *"I did and didn't want to see you, but I thought I would tell you in person that I need some time with my boys and for myself".* She also said *"I will not see you for awhile; but I will call you when I'm not such an emotional wreck, and when my life and my sons' lives are back into some sort of order. I need to feel whole again, and then our lives can move forward, hopefully together".*

With tears streaming down her face, she gave me a small kiss. An apparently broken-hearted lady got into her car and was gone.

I thought to myself, maybe if I had not gotten involved in Anne Marie's life, that just possibly the two of them could have patched up their differences. I then remembered that Anne Marie had said that her husband had another woman in his life, and that she was keeping him happy in bed. She had also stated that her husband had not wanted or touched her body in a very long time. Consequently, I was not the main factor in the pending divorce.

This gave me some momentary satisfaction since the pressure of responsibility was not on my shoulders for what was happening in her life. Then my thoughts turned to the fact that maybe I was just a convenience and the timing had just been appropriate for her and I was merely an end to justify the means.

Then my thoughts registered the rest of her conversation. She said that she needed time for herself and her sons to get their lives back to some sense of order, and would not see me for awhile. How long was awhile? How long before our regular Monday night usual sexual encounter? How long a dry spell would I have to endure?

This had been a bummer of a night. Not only had I bowled badly; but I was going to be cut off from sex with Anne Marie. But that was a nice ritual that we had put in place, and I did look forward to it. Anne Marie still came out to Monday night bowling, because she did not want to let down the team, by being further short handed. If the truth be known, as she told me later, it was nice to see me, ever so briefly. For me, Monday bowling night totally lost interest for me. Now it seemed more like a chore to complete, before the day was done.

We would make open, polite conversation with one another, but that was it. The night would end with the each of us walking separately to our cars. It was as though the whole nine yards of togetherness was just a dream. We were complete and total strangers now.

Willie was now a lot happier since I was always home at night and always sooner than before. He would always greet me with his tail wagging, eager for his nightly walk and bonding time. Our lives together were now on a more regular schedule and soon, although he did not know it, we would both be occupying a lot more of each other's time, because the bowling season was drawing to a close.

It was now mid-week and I called Erin as promised, from the office because that was the order of the day. When I finally spoke to her she said *"You sound either very down or just sad. How come"?* I was very surprised that she had picked up on my emotional state since she was not usually that perceptive, of me or my feelings. I was momentarily in a state of shock. But I quickly responded. Fortunately for me a newspaper was open to the obituary section on my desk and instantly I told her that someone in the office had died. SAVED BY THE PAPER!

We made small talk briefly and Erin said *"I feel like going to a show this weekend or possibly out to dinner. What do you think of that idea"?* I could not believe my ears. Had she just said the two of us? My God, this was a major transformation from the normal routine. I told her I was very pleased we would be going out on a date together this weekend. I was on a momentary high, but good old Erin was quick to burst my bubble.

She said *"Rebecca is busy working on report cards this weekend for her classes at school, so that it will just be the two of us"*. I really didn't want to hear that. I was in my little dream world, and actually had fooled myself to believing that maybe Erin was changing and realizing that we needed some serious time together to build our relationship stronger.

Boy, the saying goes "ONCE A FOOL, ALWAYS A FOOL" and this resounded in my head. Oh, well at least there was something to look forward to this weekend and not just a quiet weekend at home. I knew that Anne Marie was not in the picture at the moment, so no explanations were needed to her, about why I was not going to be around this weekend. With a little lighter spirit, knowing that life was not rich and full, but also not having time hang heavily on my hands this weekend, I went about the rest of the week's activities.

In a way, I was looking forward to seeing Erin again, but not with the same intensity or sensation as I had experienced the previous weekend. There would be no sex with Erin and Rebecca working on her report cards for school, so there would be no chance of a sexual rendezvous with her either. It definitely would be a dry weekend with no pleasure, and all I could do was to hope that maybe the following weekend the pleasure meter may be up and running. I was hopeful that a party to celebrate the finishing of the report cards would be something for me to anticipate. Any occasion to celebrate could be high on the list of events to happen, particularly after the quiet weekend of school reports was done.

I DEEPLY HOPED THIS WOULD BE THE CASE!

My logical mind decided I was indeed on the right course of action. The following weekend there was to be a barbeque where dinner and drinking would go hand in hand. I was hopeful that a potential get-together with Rebecca would be the icing on the cake.

I arrived late afternoon at Erin's to find the two girls busy getting drinks for everyone. As well, the barbeque was ready for the food. In her usual good form, Erin just snapped at me *"Why are you so late? You should have come earlier to help"*. I thought . . . "well nice to see you as well; glad you are finally here." That would have been a far nicer reception than the one I got! Not a pleasant welcome indeed.

I wondered why I had even come. I must be a beggar for punishment! One reason I had come was the hope of sex with Rebecca afterward.

As Erin, just like a little general, barked out orders to Rebecca and me for things she wanted done, I paused in the list of things to do. I thought how quickly I was back into the same old routine of drinking and partying. It was as if I had never left. Welcome home!

As the "fetcher", I was kept busy seeing to everyone's drinks and their refills. I watched "the little general" drinking and being the chef at the barbeque. And I watched Rebecca busy in the kitchen, getting things ready for the barbeque, hunting up paper plates and utensils for the guests. I was making small talk with Rebecca while getting the drinks and could see from her speech that she was enjoying her beverages as well. I thought that at this particular moment the night was young still and providing both the women stood their present course of drinking, my hope for a connection with Rebecca later, certainly looked promising.

My only hope was that Rebecca would not overdo the drinking and pass out. She was always the horniest after several drinks; but maybe it was just showing her true desires. Whatever the case, I was thinking that there was a better than 50/50 chance for a sexual rendezvous tonight.

By late evening, the party was over. Erin had gone to bed and was indeed passed out, long gone from this world at the moment. Rebecca was ever so gently bouncing off the walls in her attempt to assist me with cleaning up the mess after the party. When we were both headed back into the kitchen, Rebecca suddenly came over to where I was putting some items away and grabbed me by my shirt, and slurred *"I want you to take me to bed and make love to me"*. I grabbed her in my arms and started kissing her . . . first softly, then with more sensation as my hands roamed over her body. Both of us were getting excited.

As we walked upstairs to her room I told Rebecca I needed to quickly look in on Erin, to make sure she was really asleep. As I opened her bedroom door carefully, trying not to make too much noise, a loud heavy snore greeted me. I smiled a smile to myself and thought "ALL IS CLEAR". I headed to the spare bedroom where I took off all my clothes and made the bed appear that someone was in it with stuffing two pillows into the covers.

I wanted to make sure that if Erin woke, and went to check my bedroom, that all would appear normal. I was just about to go to Rebecca's bedroom when a loud knock came on the mutual bedroom wall. I was momentarily frozen and quickly slipped into Rebecca's bedroom and told her to stop because she may wake Erin.

I guess my guilty conscience must have come into play because if the truth be known, Erin was long gone and in a dead sleep. But, but still I was a little nervous. I was a little uneasy with Erin's close proximity to Rebecca's bedroom. It was playing havoc with my mind and the sounds that soon would be coming from it were a worry.

I climbed into Rebecca's bed and in the next few moments the excitement mounted quickly and all thoughts of Erin disappeared. We were both very anxious to climb that mountain of ecstasy as we roamed over and stroked each other's bodies, the intensity continuing to mount for that intimate union. We both wanted that pleasure meter to explode with the total satisfaction that the fireworks would be sending signals throughout our bodies confirming that we had indeed reached that peak of ecstasy.

Afterwards, we laid there in pools of sweat, both now breathing heavily, satisfaction glowing on our faces. We almost had the ability to light up the room. I tried to whisper into Rebecca's ear how satisfying that moment had been, and was hoping that round two may be of interest to her. I was totally surprised when I looked at the silly smile of contentment that was now on her face. But now she too had passed out. There went my plans. But hey, my plan to "put the icing on the cake of pleasure" had been achieved. I left Rebecca's bedroom a happy man and returned to my bedroom for the welcoming sleep that my body so needed now, and the pleasant dreams of moments ago.

I heard Erin wake and head for the bathroom. Shortly after she poked her head into both Rebecca's and my bedroom and told us to get up. Since "she" was up, the rest of the world should be up as well. At least this was her way of thinking. I arose as "commanded", dressed and ventured downstairs for a well needed coffee.

Erin said *"I'm hung over; finish your coffee and go home"*. I felt like replying to her "WELL GOOD MORNING TO YOU SUNSHINE", but thought better of it. Instead, I just nodded my head and left shortly after. I said goodbye to Erin but not to Rebecca because she had refused to get out of bed and was still sleeping.

I arrived home to a slightly welcome wagging from Willie, who had to sleep outside all night. I knew he was not happy with me, so I got him some fresh water and some new food and knew again I would have to work on getting back into his good graces. I took him for a long walk when he was finished with his food in an attempt to make him feel better. I was hoping for a little nap on our return home. I was still feeling a little guilty for leaving him outside all night; but took comfort in the fact that it was only one night, and not the usual routine for him.

Willie and I had a good walk and I actually felt better, more awake, more refreshed, and was not really looking forward to a nap so much as before. I played fetch with him in the backyard on our return and soon felt the grumbles of my stomach for some food as well. We went inside to look after that issue. Soon after I had eaten, I started combing Willie's coat. Again I hoped to ease my own guilty feelings about leaving him alone.

After I saw the look of happiness back on Willie's face, then I went about the normal Sunday routine of housework and laundry. I called Erin later that evening just to have some small talk and see how the rest of her day had gone. I asked about our get together next weekend and she said *"Thank you for all your help cleaning up. I hope you had a good time. You can call later in the week, and she hung up"*. Erin was all business; no kind of small talk held any interest for her. So I was not surprised at the briefness of the call. I thought "Erin if you only knew about my good time, you would be mad and definitely through with me".

Monday night was soon here . . . the very last night of bowling. Then we would wrap up with a bowling banquet as the final finish. Everyone's spirits seemed high, except for two of us. They would be announcing the trophy winners and the details of the banquet. Anne Marie and I sensed a feeling of loss. This was the very final night we would ever see each other. Bowling seemed to just fly by; we both didn't even notice what was happening through the night and all too soon it was over.

Anne Marie and I walked to our cars in almost total silence. She finally said *"I will call you"*, and with a good night wave, she was gone. I wondered what she meant with that statement," that she would call". Did it mean sooner or later? Was it just a polite way to end our relationship?

I called Erin later in the week to see if we were making any plans for the upcoming weekend. She told me that she wouldn't be around because she and Rebecca had made plans to check out the Windsor casino. Then she said *"Have a nice weekend; talk to you later."* I thought "Am I just chopped liver?" But yes, I would come at her bidding.

Again I was having feelings of loneliness; but I was used to that before the days of Anne Marie. Apparently I would have to get used to them again. I was going to have to put up with Erin and her treatment of me because it was always going to be "her way" or "the highway". I felt like I had no one in my world again, and Erin was my last resort for any female companionship. In my mind's way of thinking, it seemed my only choice. NOT TOO LOGICAL ON MY PART!

Willie was a least happy to have me around so much! I contented myself with his time and love, and so another weekend would come and go without female companionship. I had made up my mind not to call Erin. I would have some backbone for a change. So the next week dragged on and no call from Erin seemed to be apparent. It was almost quitting time on Friday, when my phone rang. It was Erin. She wanted to know if I would like to come over after work for a drink and I said *"Sounds like a plan".* But what I really wanted to say was "OH, YOU HAVE TIME FOR ME NOW. HOW KIND OF YOU"! If I <u>had</u> said that, I might just as well have put a nail in my coffin, because there would definitely be another weekend alone. I went over to Erin's, only to find it full of people already there drinking. They would just be ordering in pizza for dinner later. How charming I thought. You were able to think about me, and to ask me over. HOW SPECIAL!

I was a total idiot for going over thinking something good was finally going to come out of a week of not seeing each other. But I had to conceal my feelings from Erin. I was mad at myself for coming; so the best thing for me to do was to tell Erin that I had business to do on Saturday and I did not want to drink too much. I had to go home in the early evening.

Erin said *"Just do whatever you want to do".* Apparently she really didn't care one way or another. I called Saturday but there was no answer, so I left a message and hoped she would return my call. It was not forthcoming!

She called late Sunday morning and said *"My Mom would like you to come for Sunday lunch. See you there."* But she did not say she was sorry for not returning my phone call, or why she was busy on Saturday. She didn't even want me to pick her up to take her to her mother's. Probably it was her Mom who wanted me there, not Erin. She probably wouldn't have even called otherwise.

When I arrived at her parent's home, I was greeted by Erin at the doorway and she said *"I was not happy with you last Friday night. You seemed angry, so I didn't even want to be around you"*. NO KIDDING! Erin had actually been very perceptive; I didn't know she had the ability. I wondered why it was alright for her to leave me high and dry the previous weekend and for her and Rebecca to go to Casino Windsor? Why was it alright not to call me through the week, and then at the last moment on Friday before work was done, to call? Why was it alright to already have a house full of people there drinking when I arrived? I thought she wanted to see only me. BUT HOW DARE I GET MAD? GO FIGURE!!

I tried my best to be friendly and outgoing during lunch, and even helped with clean up and dishes afterwards. I felt so unwanted. I was told that she and Rebecca were going to wash their cars after lunch. Since I was not invited to join them, I took the hint; thanked her parents for a lovely lunch and then drove home. It was going to be another long week with no Erin. I would just have to wait till her state of mind changed and then she might call. To say our relationship was a little rocky would be the understatement of all time. She finally called two weeks later, as though nothing had happened . . . at least to her way of thinking.

When Erin called she asked me if I wanted to go to the show that coming weekend. I said *"I would love to and that it was great to hear from her again"*. What I truly wanted to say was "And just who is calling? Do you have the right phone number?" That would have been suicidal for me. I guess in her own small way this was Erin's way of apologizing. She would never use that word and she never apologized very often.

We set a time for me to go over to her home since she had already picked out the movie we were to see and the plans were already set. We actually had a good evening together and we shared good conversation, something we had not done in a long time. I was even stunned at the end of the evening when she kissed me good night. She then said for me to come over early on Saturday. A group of them was going to the Legion to have some drinks and a good afternoon.

I couldn't believe my ears. Erin actually sounded like she wanted my company and wanted me to enjoy the day with her and her friends.

It all sounded too good, to be true, but I didn't want to rock the boat. I said *"I would really enjoy being with you on Saturday."* It was like we were starting a fresh new relationship. Again I was hopeful as well as happy that we were moving forward, seemingly on a positive note.

The weekend was the best we had had in years; it really did feel like we were bonding to one another with a special closeness. It was something we had not felt for each other in a very long time. I was thrilled with this new Erin, and a future seemed to be on the horizon for us. I had waited many years for this lady, and now the moment seemed to have arrived.

She seemed to have a whole new attitude, outlook and desire, as well as a whole new image. It was like the other side of a coin was now showing itself to me. It appeared that Erin had finally arrived at the feeling of wanting to settle down with me, and start a life together. These wishes of mine had now finally materialized. I was not sure at this very moment in my life if I was dreaming or was it truly reality. Many years of waiting and hoping for this time to arrive was now at hand. The thought that was going through my head was "All good things come to those who wait" and I so hoped this was the case.

I even volunteered to be the designated driver to see that everyone arrived home safely. I thought that this was good logic as then I could drive home myself. I didn't want to be tempted by Rebecca calling me to her bedroom. All things in my world seemed at this very moment, to be right on track for a future with Erin. I didn't want to jeopardize this opportunity by being caught while I was in Rebecca's bed. It was the right thing to do for me to just go home, and not venture to that zone of pleasure.

Just as my world with Erin had finally taken shape and my future seemed bright, that Sunday morning there a knock came to my door. I was momentarily surprised by the sound. When I opened the door I saw Anne Marie standing there. I was stunned and speechless. She said *"Are you not going to ask me in?"* and then she laughed. She said *"You look like you have seen a ghost, and I am definitely not a ghost"*.

I told her that I wasn't sure that I would ever see her again. She responded with *"I told you I would call you; but I decided I would rather see you instead because I have missed you"*. Anne Marie came in and because I was doing my usual Sunday morning chores of house cleaning and laundry just wearing my housecoat, I apologized to her for not being dressed.

She said *"I remember something you said when I was wearing your housecoat the weekend I stayed with you. You said that it looked better on me than you. You also said that there was less clothing to take off before we went to bed".* Then she laughed and said *"That clothing item applies to you as well. That is why I came out to your home to have you take me to bed. I need to feel you inside me, your kisses and making love with you. It has been so long".*

Well, not being one to turn down an opportunity, I locked the door, and we headed arm in arm down the hallway and upstairs to the bedroom. Anne Marie was indeed anxious to get in bed as she flung open my housecoat, all the while pushing me towards the bed. She was instantly upon me, roaming her hands over my body, and I was instantly thrown into a frenzy of excitement. My hands were pulling and tugging at her clothing, and she was busy helping me. We were soon there nude, side by side. Both of us were longing to feel the other's body, wanting to explore special spots, all the while the excitement of the forthcoming pleasure beginning to reach an explosive point. The peak of ecstasy was reached almost instantly as our bodies fused! The fireworks, the bells, the whistles all resounded in what seemed a heartbeat, because neither of us could wait a second longer. Anne Marie said *"That happened too quickly; but I think we each missed the sex with one another. I am so looking forward to round two because I know what you are capable of".*

As well, I was not satisfied with the quick sex and was hopeful that she was not in a hurry to get home. I looked forward to sex with Anne Marie for the rest of the day, if possible. She said *"I can only stay a couple hours, and I am hopeful that it will be long enough for both of us to be fully satisfied".* We laid there in our pool of sweat, hugging one another, not wanting to let go and hopeful that time would stand still. We were both happy at the moment and we did indeed have a couple of hours of slow, passionate love-making. But instead of time standing still, it seemed to be galloping on and all too soon it was time for her to leave.

Anne Marie said *"I will call you later tonight to talk, because when we are together all we do is have sex. Talking takes a back seat to the pleasure at hand".* I walked her to her car, and yes I was still in my housecoat when

I gave her a kiss, a wave, and she was homeward bound. I thought how wonderful a Sunday afternoon this was! I could see no point in this late hour of the day in getting dressed but a final walk with Willie would still be needed.

Anne Marie called later that evening and we talked about some small issues before she got into the main reason for her call. She said *"I want to live with you. I want for me and my two sons to start a full-time life together with you and to finally be a whole family unit. I want total happiness for me"*. I was totally taken aback at this thought and silence reigned as my brain mulled over all the information that I had just heard.

Anne Marie said *"What have you to say for yourself? Why are you so silent"?* I told her that I really wanted to be with her; but I wasn't sure of the "family package deal". She said *"Well it is me and my two sons or nothing."* I said *"I was in a terrible first marriage with Amy and her children and that had not worked out. You already know this! I am not ready for children to be part of my life. I can't cope with it. I don't like being in the third position of importance. This is where you will put me."* Anne Marie said *"It wouldn't have to be like that at all. You merely have to go along with the situation of my children being around. I will never put you in third position of importance"*. I replied *"Unfortunately, it would just come naturally with your motherly instincts, and you won't even be aware of it happening"*.

At this point Anne Marie was crying and I was also upset with myself for saying these things; but I knew in my heart that having her young sons around me daily would not work for me. I was very selfish with my time and my possessions. I would eventually start to regret even trying such a relationship. It would just be like a runaway train heading for an inevitable train wreck! Why would I even consider putting myself in that situation of having to break up my home? It would cost me a lot of money to do so.

This didn't make any sense to me to go that route whatsoever. However, my sex life would be fantastic and probably daily, until the inevitable break-up. Initially, daily sex would have been the only good point in the proposed living accommodations that came to my mind. But in the end, I would not come out ahead overall.

Anne Marie was still crying and said to me *"Is this your final decision? You will not change your attitude or your thinking on this issue"?* I told her that I could not see how it would possibly ever work out with the three of them moving in with me.

There was dead silence on the telephone! My world with her was now totally over, and sadness did overtake me. My thoughts were that my words and my deeds for shattering yet another heart were totally <u>my</u> fault. I knew I had led her on to the possibility of a life together with me.

In reality she was as much to blame for hanging her hopes and dreams on me. She was already aware of my previous attempt at a family and married life. It was her decision and her ex-husband's wishes to separate. It took the two of them to tango and to reach that point in their lives, even before I entered the picture. I was trying to ease my state of mind with what had just taken place. Now I was looking to release my guilty feelings, and not let them totally take me into depression.

I knew in my heart that it was the best for all concerned to end it now. I just had to concentrate all my time and effort into building a firm relationship with Erin. I had a strong feeling in both my mind and heart that Erin was now sincere about wanting to start a life with me, and it needed to start with a clean slate for it to work out.

I knew I had given up a great sex partner with Anne Marie; but lust had been the driving force in my desire to be with her. As they say "I had made my bed and I had to live with my decision". I had always wanted Erin from the very beginning of my many previous relationships. For me now, my dream was about to be realized, so I was going with my heart's direction. I was sincerely hoping with everything in me, that happiness was on my doorstep and my dream life with Erin had finally arrived.

HAD I MADE A BIG MISTAKE?

Erin seemed more intent with phone calls to me, wanting to spend more private time together but there was no sex. She said that once we were married that would change. For a few months this seemed to be the pattern . . . enjoying time with her and our friends; but still I still felt like I had to keep pinching myself.

That Christmas I asked Erin to marry me and we had already been shopping for a wedding ring. This seemed the appropriate time to propose to Erin. At the Christmas dinner at her parent's home, we made the announcement of our forthcoming wedding. A joyous Christmas had been enriched with this news. Hugs, kisses and handshakes were given by all except Rebecca. All she offered was a handshake! This left a momentary coldness in me because I was not sure if she was not happy with the news. I was glad she felt she had to be polite anyway. I could not really put my finger on it, but an uncomfortable feeling left its mark on me.

Erin wanted a June wedding and that was also her birthday month. That would be good for me to remember cards for both occasions in the same month. It would also give us a good six months to organize the wedding and to save up for the expenses that we would be accruing. Erin had decided we both would contribute largely to the total cost of the wedding.

I always thought that the bride's parents had that responsibility. I thought the costs for their daughter's wedding would be theirs. But we would have to contribute something towards it. At least that's what I remembered from other people's weddings.

Erin as "the little general" was once again showing her true colours. She was now in total command, and I was a mere "buck private". I would be taking the orders as issued and in my stupidity decided to allow her to do things her way. But because I also wanted everything to be done perfectly, I hoped I would have some input into the wedding plans.

I MIGHT HAVE BEEN IN A SMALL BUBBLE AT THIS MOMENT!!

Erin had decided that we would get married in the Catholic Church and I really didn't care one way or another. The first problem arose because I had been previously married. It seemed to cause an issue in the Catholic faith. Apparently, this is a big NO! NO!

We had to jump through a lot of hoops to find a priest who would marry us. Erin had finally pinned one down and we were to have our first meeting with him that very night. Erin introduced me to him as Father Michael, and told me to call him such. Without even thinking, I said that he wasn't my father that I thought I would just call him "Mike".

The look I got from Erin could have stopped an eight-day clock. But hey! That was how I felt about the situation. TOO BAD!!

This was my first mistake in meeting the minister. But Father Michael said to Erin that he had no problem with me calling him

Mike. Soon Erin's ruffled feathers were starting to settle down. The wedding programme was set in motion, and all the people involved had been contacted for the day's event. The music had been selected, and the dry run for the wedding itself was in place.

Erin then decided we would have the wedding dinner at the Wayside Dining Lounge. Consequently we paid a visit to select the meal for our big day. Erin also thought that as my home was in the village of Talbotville, we would have the reception party there. I had a large two storey home with finished areas in both the basement and the garage. It would no doubt work ideally for the day's event.

We could set up the tables in the garage area for the dinner later in the evening, and the basement would work out for the drinking, partying, and dancing area. I also had a larger wooden deck and patio area for people to use and enjoy. Seemingly, Erin had thought this whole process through. The last order of the day was for each of us to start buying alcohol for the party, each time we got paid, until we had as much as we thought we would need. It seemed no stone had been left unturned by Erin, who was acting like the "wedding planner General". All I had to do was to go along with her plans. It was "almost like going along for the ride" until the big day finally arrived. Life seemed to be going along very smoothly during these six months of preparation. Erin actually seemed totally excited with the whole concept and total happiness was the tune of the day!

The big day finally arrived; the weather co-operated, and no speed bumps loomed the whole day. My gut was telling me it all seemed too perfect. The people arriving seemed happy and looking forward to the wedding and the celebrations that would follow.

There was only one person who was not totally sure what was about to happen. Self doubt was now rearing its ugly head as I was getting dressed in my tuxedo and waiting for my parents to arrive. My gut feeling that something was not quite right with the whole occasion now faced me head-on. I was now second guessing myself about what I was about to do with my life.

I had waited nineteen years to get to this point. All the years of hurt feelings, cancellation of plans, being totally forgotten, messages being ignored and her quick temper were all now in the forefront of my mind. Erin had always demanded that things go her way! The lack of any physical connection and her being able to turn emotions on and off at will, were the thoughts that were now dancing in my head.

Doubt was kicking in about what I was going to do this very day. Happy thoughts were not among any of my concerns for the wedding that was looming almost too closely, at this very moment. When my parents finally arrived, they sensed my concern and so we sat down and had a discussion about my feelings. I was totally open with them; but they just chalked it up to nervousness on my part. They said it was to be expected with the groom on his wedding day. They said it would pass once we arrived at the church. I would then reaffirm in my mind that indeed this was "my day" that I had wished for all those years, and the "funny" feelings would totally disappear.

In hindsight, I wish I had listened to my gut and my brain as they had both been working overtime trying to get me to see the light about the rocky road that lay ahead for me. There was a totally shattered heart on the horizon; but I am getting ahead of my story.

The wedding ceremony and the picture-taking all seemed lost to me. The people I talked to later, all concluded that I seemed to be in my right mind during the whole procedure. I smiled when I was told to do so and even signed where I was directed to. I even seemed to be able to walk down the aisle without stopping or falling down. OH GOD A MARRIED MAN! What had I just done to myself? These thoughts were racing through my mind, as I was told to smile for the camera.

I had rented a limousine for our ride as a married couple to the Wayside Dining Lounge. Thoughts of the open bar loomed in my head. I needed a stiff drink to calm me down, to shake off this feeling, to get into the reality of just what had happened to me. People were constantly arriving; the alcohol flowed freely; the smiles and party atmosphere was aglow.

After a fine meal, toasts given, pictures and speeches completed, I rose to announce the party would follow at "our" new home. Everyone could follow the limousine to where it was going to be held. All in all, the party, the drinking and the whole wedding reception party seemed to be taking its natural course. Everyone was enjoying the festivities, except me.

My gut feeling was still with me, and was increasing hour by hour. As the last guests were leaving, everyone wanted to say a final congratulation to the bride, before they headed home.

I had not seen too much of Erin from the time we arrived at "home". I merely thought that she had been busy with guests as I had been. We had been like "ships passing in the night". My gut finally told me to go upstairs and look into the bedroom. O. M. G.!

The lovely bride was drunk and passed out on the bed. How wonderful for this special night and our union as a married couple!!! I could not believe my eyes! Why on this of all nights had she gotten so drunk?

As I was walking down the stairway I spotted Rebecca and asked her to put Erin to bed, and to clean her up. Rebecca just laughed at me and said *"She is now your problem MR. Groom"*, but finally agreed to do as I had asked.

Finally everyone had gone and as I looked around at the total mess that was left behind, I couldn't believe my eyes. Erin's parents and sister had said they would come out the next day to help with the cleanup so I was not to worry. *"Welcome to the family"* was their last comment as they went out the door.

My mind told me there was no sense in going to the bedroom with a passed out, drunken bride. I might just as well get started on the cleanup of the mess as it totally bothered me anyway. I worked throughout the whole night, cleaning up, washing dishes. The whole nine yards of activities were seen through to completion.

Daylight was now beginning to show, and being totally exhausted, I went to the couch and fell instantly asleep. I was not sure of their arrival because I didn't feel like I had slept very long, but there was a knock at the door. Erin's parents and sister had arrived to start the cleaning up.

They were amazed at me as I was still dressed in my tuxedo from the day before and truly looked like "death warmed over". I struggled to ask them in, said that I would make some coffee and get Erin up. I am not sure what her parents and sister thought but they all said *"Paul, you have cleaned the whole house and even did the dishes!"*

I tried my best to say that I thought it was my responsibility. What I really wanted to say was "Your daughter was drunk and she passed out. What did you expect me to do on my wedding night"? I will always remember that I spent it cleaning the house and "NOT consolidating the Marriage". WHAT A GREAT MEMORY!

Erin came down the stairway having put on her best face for her parents. But it was definitely not for the new husband! I am sure, given the chance, she would have loved to stay in bed by herself for the rest of the day. Erin gave a non emotional response to my *"good morning Hon,"* as she barked to me, *"Have you got the coffee made?"* I nodded my head "yes".

Erin and her family ventured into the family room to wait for the delivery of the coffee from the "coffee man" (also now known as waiter, husband or groom). Upon my arrival, Erin was busy opening wedding cards and gifts. They were all saying how nice that so and so relative from the United States had sent a nice gift of money, as had most of the relatives from the States.

I never ever heard the total amount of money that was received and I never ever saw a dime of it. It was as though it never existed to me, at least from Erin's point of view.

She was enjoying opening the gifts and her sister was recording who they were from for the thank you cards to be forwarded in response. I was busy refilling coffee mugs and picking up pieces of paper that were lying around on the floor from the unwrapped gifts. I thought "I may never know who gave what as a gift and as it appears it doesn't really matter. I should just keep doing what I was doing and see to everyone's needs".

It was as though I was in my own right mind on the outside of all that was happening. No one even paid any attention and for that matter seemed to care. My gut instinct had been right, this was a marriage made in HELL and I might be in this for the long run. It would be my decision to decide my own fate.

After Erin's parents and sister had left, she said to me *"I'm going back to bed. Thanks for cleaning up the house. See you later"*. I could not have gotten any colder a response than that. Welcome to Marriage with Erin!

We did not have any money left after we paid for our wedding. When Monday rolled around, we were both off to work, as though it had just been another party weekend. She didn't come home for supper that night and when she did finally arrive she simply said *"I dropped into Rebecca's and she asked me to stay for supper. Sorry I didn't call. I guess I am not used to this marriage life routine yet"*.

We both struggled to enjoy married life; but there was definitely something major lacking. From my prospective point of view it was a big problem. There was no communication, no sex and no involvement with one another. NOTHING!

We were simply living under the same roof, but living separate lives. Erin didn't like the drive from Talbotville to London to go to work each day, or to have to go back there to see her friends. This became a constant bone of contention between us. She did not like Willie or even having him presence in the house. This too became a major fighting issue between us.

It seemed mutual from Willie's point of view as well. Who could really blame him for his good sense of judgement? Their dislike for one another was very apparent.

OH MY GOD! WHAT IS HAPPENING IN MY WORLD? Erin was constantly looking at real estate booklets. This soon became part of our every day topic of discussion, along with whatever else had dared to rock her world. She had finally worn me down to the point of having to protect my sanity. I agreed to sell the home and move to London. Erin said *"I would really like to have a home built as our first home together and to have it built in Lambeth"*.

I thought originally that Erin may be right. This had been my home before Erin came to live here, so likely Erin did not feel this was her home. I also thought naively, that if we built a home we would bond together in the process. Erin would then feel like this was now "home" for the both of us.

I listed the home and to my surprise it sold quickly, so we were forced to find another property before the closing date on our current residence arrived. Fortunately for us the new owners agreed to a long closing date to allow us to build our new home. We found a vacant lot in Lambeth Estates, just across from Greenhill Golf and Country Club.

We picked out a house plan we liked and I added some interior design features that she was not even aware of, but surprisingly really liked them. The final added feature that I included was to purchase the brick for the house exterior from the torn down train round house station in St. Thomas. They were up for sale and there was enough quantity to meet our total demands.

In this small way, I would have a piece of St. Thomas heritage for our home, and the full brick wall interior of our family room would have the same brickwork. As the home completion was continuing forward, Erin dropped another bomb on me. She didn't want Willie to come with us. *"Give him to the neighbours; let him live his life out in the country."*

My heart was totally shattered. This was my best friend. She had now laid down the law and it was the first I knew how she really felt about Willie. My best friend was no longer welcome in our new home. I was upset, furious, and totally saddened by this news. How could Erin be so cruel and so mean? I knew they both did not like each other; but never in my wildest dreams did I think this would ever be demanded by Erin. But I was at a crossroads.

I was married to Erin and she would get 50% from the sale of the house. I would have to go to an apartment to live, if I wanted Willie to live with me.

MY WORLD WAS SHATTERED ONCE AGAIN!

I talked with my neighbour Walter, who had been my foreman on work projects, as well as a good friend to me. I told him about my situation with Willie and Erin's dislike for him. Walter said *"Willie is getting quite slow in his old age, and wouldn't demand too much walking at night. My yard is enclosed as well, so it would not be a problem for Willie to live the rest of his life here with my wife and me."*

I stopped in my thinking process momentarily because I had never really noticed how old Willie was and how much he really had slowed down. He was always happy to see me, a small play, a small walk, and then he was contented to just lay on the floor while I brushed him, much to Erin's disgust.

I guess when you see your best friend on a daily basis you don't seem to notice how old he is getting and only see him through kind eyes and remember what a great dog he is.

Erin was either on the phone or had gone to bed alone. What did it really matter to her how I spent evenings with Willie? I would go to bed whenever I got around to it, usually after Willie's final walk of the evening. Since Erin still did not like sex, it would merely be to go to sleep anyway. Why is having Willie live with us such a big issue for her?

It was either Erin's way or the highway. So when moving day finally arrived, I moved Willie next door with tears in my eyes and we moved to Lambeth. The only saving grace was that I knew how much Willie would be loved by Walter and his wife I knew in my heart they would give him a great home life and see to his every need.

I AM SORRY WITH ALL MY HEART FOR LEAVING YOU, WILLIE!

The new home, the new life, the now-realized dreams of Erin about her new home didn't seem to make an impact on our marriage, or our living arrangement. She told me I could have the master bedroom as she liked the other large bedroom and the furniture, she had recently bought. It would fit in there quite well. My facial expression must have said it all.

Erin said to me *"Now we can have our own separate bedrooms and bathrooms, and we won't be in each other's way getting ready for bed or for getting ready to go to work"*.

There was no other comment like . . . you live in your space and I will live in mine. I thought this might be the finishing statement out of her mouth. She was a cold fish and I had been played "like a fish". If I had a gun at that moment I would have just shot myself.

This was the misery I had put myself into, my future and now my life style. Existing this way was not a pleasant thought, and I longed for a quick way out. Somehow I had been foolish enough to believe that complying with Erin's demands and fulfilling her requests, somehow life would be on a different scale. In the far corner of my brain I believed that the new house, new location and new bond of togetherness would be the kick off to a great married life!

BOY, WHAT A BUBBLE MY SIMPLE MIND MUST HAVE BEEN IN?

Erin was to have her world and mine would be whatever I could make myself. We were still and always would be two people living under the same roof and living two separate lives.

THIS IS NOT WHAT I SIGNED ON FOR, NOR WHAT I EVEN WANTED FOR THE REST OF MY LIFE!!

I would come home from work, and most likely Erin would not be there. Nor would there be any note from her. She would simply come home, change and be gone who knows where. I never knew what time she would return. Initially I used to make enough supper for the two of us. But I quickly learned she ate at Rebecca's, her mother's or elsewhere. She didn't want to bother with any meal preparations.

Life was lonely. I didn't have any time with Erin. When she did come home, we would talk briefly, and then she would go to her bedroom. I didn't even have my Willie for company. I didn't have anyone to love or to love me back.

I raised the subject of getting a pet. Erin responded angrily and I was told *"NO WAY, NOT IN THIS HOUSE!"* So the issue was dead. I was basically living alone, waiting for a complete stranger to pass through the hallway on her route to her bedroom. I spent many nights talking to myself. I kept asking over and over again, "WHAT THE HELL WAS I DOING LIVING HERE, LIVING WITH A GHOST"? I was now in total despair, full of unhappiness, and completely alone. These were my new "companions". There was a fourth. There was TV, to break up the night and to put voices in the house. I thought "YOU ARE A COMPLETE FOOL"! You have a house but no home; you have a woman but no wife. You are very much alone. There is no company, no warmth and no love in your life.

"How" I kept asking myself? "Why" I kept asking myself? "Who" I kept asking myself, "is this woman, that I have for years totally control my thoughts, my actions, my deeds and my life?" What had been such a drawing card for this person? Why had I let a single person have total control, to make her my life, my top priority? Why had I sold myself, my soul and my very spirit, to such an unloving, unfeeling, piece of clay?

God had created this woman, and she had turned out to be my Eve in the Garden of Eden. Obviously God was not happy with me. I was not to know real happiness, love, contentment, and a full life with a single woman. It seemed all my life, I had made wrong decisions with women, and had been involved with the wrong women, and had made poor choices in my life. Why had I not the ability to think clearly about what I was doing and about the life pathway I was choosing?

I was utterly and completely and totally a mixed up person. Logic and common sense never seemed to come into play when I was getting involved or was involved with any woman.

IT WAS AS THOUGH GOD WAS PUNISHING ME, AND THIS WAS MY HELL ON EARTH!!

Erin and I drifted through more months of tolerating each other's presence in life. I always had to put on my best face, and put my best foot forward, when in her family's company. There were the family dinners, family occasions and time with her friends. But for the most part, we drove in separate cars to these events so that Erin could go back to Rebecca's or simply dismiss me to go home. I would go back alone to the empty house and to an empty existence like someone on a vacant island. I was growing tired of all the charades of appearing as a couple. However, most people knew all along, except for me, that Erin would never change. I would have to accept this lifestyle.

I told myself that I needed to get some "BALLS" and say that "ENOUGH IS ENOUGH". I wanted out! I knew that I had wasted many years of trying, hoping, praying and wishing that Erin and I would have a great life together.

BOY! HOW THICK HEADED CAN ONE FOOL BE?

One Saturday when Erin was actually there to do both the laundry and the ironing, I told her that I was very unhappy with our life and the way we were living. I said *"Either you try to make a go of our marriage with more effort, and start including me far more in your life or I want a divorce".* She finally said *"The only reason I wanted to get married was because of the rumours at the hospital, that I was a lesbian. I wanted them stopped and marriage was the only way to do it, even though it was true".*

You could have knocked me down with a feather! I was totally dumbfounded! I had always thought there was a possibility she might be one, but never brought up the subject. There never seemed an appropriate time. In fact would you even bring up the topic with your girlfriend or your wife?

Finally the light switch in my brain and in my life got turned on! The question had finally been answered. The suspicions, the gut feeling had all been addressed with this statement. Finally SHE HAD COME OUT OF THE CLOSET! I was totally speechless and my life and my heart now lay crumbled and in tatters on the ground

OH! MY! GOD! Was all that kept repeating itself over and over inside my head? No wonder she was so protective of Rebecca, who must have been a switch hitter. But all the hurt, anger and sorrow now showed my total stupidity. How could I be attracted to a lesbian? What in God's name had been the attraction? Was I so totally naïve? Why was

I so forgiving of Erin and her treatment of me? Why had I done this to myself for all these years?

I guess I may never know the reasons for thinking like this; but I realized that Erin knew how to play me like a fiddle to get what she wanted all along. The only reason for the whole marriage and years of dating all were because of comments from co-workers and the lifestyle she was living. So I guess in the end I was useful! I had released her from all the idle comments through my very existence and the marriage been the final proof. I am glad however, that one of us got something positive out of all the years of "pretend"!

As a great political thinker had once stated "the end justifies the means" and now I truly understand the meaning of that statement. I had lived it and breathed it for many years. The end was now at hand. I would again be on my own. In reality however, I had been alone all along. I just now finally realized it and facing the truth <u>does</u> hurt. I could finally wake up and smell the roses and wait for the divorce proceedings.

Again Erin would lay her final bomb on me. I met her and her father at their lawyer's, supposedly to do the arrangements and do the initial signing of all the paperwork. That wasn't quite going to be the case. Erin said she would take all the profit money from the house sale, plus 50% of the household contents but she would not touch my valuable art collection **if** I would agree to her terms. A broken-spirited man, a disheartened man, a foolish man agreed to her terms and signed the paperwork. Just like that, my time with Erin was done.

I was now left to do the sale of the house, make up the proper apportionments of furniture and the final cleanup of the house after it sold. In hindsight, I should have told Erin's lawyer that we never had sex in the marriage and I would get my lawyer to fight the terms that had been set down. This would have cost me a lot more money and lawyers would be the only ones that came out smelling like roses. In reality, I just wanted it done and completed as soon as possible. The quicker I got away from Erin, the better. So there was no point in bringing sex into play.

As the saying goes "Go with the flow and move on". I am not sure at this point what to move on to. I must venture into the unknown, and see what life might have to offer. There is a saying that I heard in my life that goes like this . . . "They say that life is not about waiting for the storm to pass. It is about caring and loving your relatives and friends, while you still can touch and see them and they are still among us". These are good words to live by and to realize their importance in one's life.

My life at the moment was totally shattered and there seemed no joy or happiness or any point to moving forward. That is when I remembered that phrase and took heart in its meaning.

I must now take on the roll of a fighter because I had lived the life of a loser for far too long. I didn't care for it and the feelings that accompanied it either. I must now try to be smarter in my selection of a girlfriend/partner; to learn to walk before I ran into a relationship; to go slowly and easily into life's unknown. If I was looking for happiness and hopefully a life's soul-mate, then these steps should be implemented as soon as possible because time stands still for no one, and I did not want to die a lonely, old man.

To this end I thought of some words of inspiration to motivate me in my quest.

I long to be able to walk in sunshine;
To show kindness to all those I meet,
Even though I may carry a burden
That many cannot see.
If life has given me reasons
To cry and carry pain;
Then I must long for the pathway
To smile and find life again.

The SECOND SEGMENT of my life has now drawn to a close. I like to think of my life as a comparison to the four seasons of a year.

THE SPRING SEASON: Life begins. You walk, talk, and observe all that life throws your way. You experience life and all its challenges, its total ups and downs, the rights and wrongs. All of these are involved in the learning curve that life offers and denies.

THE SUMMER SEASON: You are now in your 20's, 30's, and 40's. You have met and lost relationships. You have enjoyed the bonds of union to woman's body. You have loved, lost, and shattered their hearts and yours. You have known pleasure, sorrow, love, and pain. You have never had a long commitment, but have enjoyed many promises, many dreams. However, there is no lasting bond to someone as soul-mate.

THE FALL SEASON: You are still in your 40's, 50's and 60's. You are still searching, longing for commitment to a special lady, a special bond, security, love and happiness that seems to have passed you by. The search continues, the desire, the need still pulsating ever so strongly. You do not want to be totally alone. That special commitment still burns in your heart for someone to be a part of your life.

THE WINTER SEASON: You are now in your 60's, 70's, and 80's. You have at this stage the strong hope of having a partner in your life. You long for that "soul-mate", and best friend. You long for that special lady to be there, to care, to share the happy moments, and all life's memories. As I have stated, you need to walk in the sunshine of both your lives, to walk the final pathway of being together here on earth, as it comes to an end. YOUR SPIRITS WOULD BE UNITED FOR ALL ETERNITY.

I was now entering the FALL of my life. I was now alone, very unhappy, totally unfulfilled, and merely just existing day to day. I had not yet adjusted to being a non-existent entity, one who merely is taking up space and air; but not one who was enjoying life.

I would join with different fellow employees at coffee break or lunch hours, just to enjoy the pleasure of hearing about other people's lives, their weekend plans, as well their vacation plans. In a small way, I was able to live in their lives and activities which gave me a connection to another human being. I was still trying to muster up the desire to join a dating service, or be willing to get matched up with an employee's friend, to get back into the dating game.

I was still longing to find that single person to share my life with and to have the opportunity to build present and future memories with a special someone. It was during one of these morning coffee breaks that I sat with a bunch of ladies from the secretarial pool. Initially, I was a little out of my element as the topic was around meal preparation, suitable dresses for certain occasions, and their children's behaviour at home and at school.

I listened in awe at how well these ladies addressed each of these topics and seemingly all were coming up with the same similar ideas for solutions. As the coffee break was drawing to a close, a couple of ladies apologized that I had not been able to get into the conversation;

but they said to please join them again. They would try to make the discussion more interesting. They said they would try their best to include me in more relevant subjects of interest and see if they couldn't spice it up some.

The two ladies that had asked me to join them again said that because I was a newcomer to the discussion group, it took a little time for everyone to feel comfortable with opening up to broader scopes of office gossip, and to put down some of the management polices and procedures.

I thanked them and said that I would like to join them again for another coffee break and was looking forward to some interesting comments from them. I further stated that I was really interested in the office gossip and thought it might prove to be very entertaining. The next day I did join the same group of ladies at coffee break and to my astonishment found that I was now a part of the group. How quickly I was taken into their confidence.

The topic was more controversial about who was sleeping with whom, who was sleeping their way up the ladder to a supervisor's position and which manager was good and which one was bad. I was amazed about how much these ladies knew about all the staff members. I was also surprised about how much in advance they knew about what new policies and procedures were going to be implemented and when that would happen. I guess it really was no mystery, since they were the people doing the typing; so why wouldn't they be aware of all the news and who was creating all the changes.

I thought that I had landed in a very good source of information and how beneficial it could prove to be. I only had to keep my ears open and my mouth shut on the sources of information that were readily at hand. As time went on, the ladies became totally relaxed in my company, and my non-harmful comments were kept within the group. Consequently, it was turning out to be a win-win situation for me.

For the moment, I was not going to be surprised with any new policies and procedures, since I was always braced and ready for the move or change in any direction. Office staff members were constantly changing. Sometimes it was totally new people joining the ranks and quite often, some were friends or friends of friends who got the new employee position. It was during one of these occasions that Wendy was hired for the secretarial pool and how my life was about to change.

From this point onward my world was to go from wrong side down, to right side up. I took an instant liking to this lady, as though some outside forces were pushing me into her direction. I offered no resistance to the forces at work, as an obvious desire to know this lady had totally consumed me. I had an instant desire to be in her company and for the life of me I could not understand what was happening to my feelings, or why I had such a strong attraction.

I looked forward to the daily coffee breaks with the ladies from the secretarial pool because I knew that Wendy would be among them. These ladies took new employees under their wing, because seemingly, they were the self-appointed official welcoming committee to all new arrivals. They acted like bees going to gather pollen to bring back to the hive, in their quest to gather information with a flurry of constant questions for the group to savour.

I think likely there was a twofold reason for their actions. One was an appreciation for new subject information or gossip. The other was to share information about what had happened to the previous employee. Secondly, they were interested to find out who this new employee knew in the organization that had got them their current position, whether it might have been a family member, friend or friend of a friend.

God forbid that they had achieved this position on their own merit and skills, as some of these ladies were old-timers and had bitter memories of being passed over by new employees. This newly discovered information would allow the group to know who they could talk about and what they could say about another fellow employee, to not step on toes or feelings. I thought how clever these ladies worked on information gathering. It all seemed quite innocent out in the open; but in reality it was C Y A (cover your ass).

A slip of your tongue might land you in the lap of the person about whom you were speaking incorrectly and there could be reprisals for your words. Life in the office could become very unpleasant. I had now seen with my own eyes how this close network of ladies in the coffee group actually worked, and it was crystal clear to me that even I should be on my best behaviour. The possibility of these ladies turning on me could be a reality, so I was definitely not too free with my comments about people in the office.

I appeared to just be a good listener. It was the safest route to avoid being kicked out of the group. Worse than that, comments could reach the wrong ears from a slip of my tongue without thinking.

This logical process appeared to be the safest route to take. To put it another way, it would be "politically correct" for me to follow this route in thought, word and deed. It was quite obvious that there was a strong possibility that "Loose Lips Sink Ships". It would not be very beneficial to have something I said come back to haunt me or for me to wait a pending reprisal that would be forthcoming.

The first few weeks of coffee breaks were quite enjoyable, because I had taken my own advice, and had only been a good listener. All the ladies constantly questioned Wendy on a variety of topics concerning her past and present life, and a wealth of information had been given. I was getting a lot of detailed information that initially, I wouldn't have had the nerve to ask but was definitely interested in learning. I heard about her history in the work world, her family life, where she had gone to school, where she had previously lived, and even of her pending divorce.

The ladies were after it all, leaving no stone unturned. I was like a sponge trying to absorb all this information so that when I had the nerve to ask her out, there was ample knowledge about her to draw on, in our first outing together. One day when the coffee break was over, and the entire group was returning to their office work stations, I approached Wendy and asked if she would like to go out for a drink after work. I said it didn't have to be today but sometime in the near future if that would be more convenient. She said *"I will think on it and let you know"*.

Here is when the bomb was about to fall on me. As I had stated earlier, the ladies' coffee break club, that I had joined, was about to turn on me with their comments and the knowledge they thought they had on me and my make-up. Wendy had told one of the ladies that I had asked her out for a drink and that she wasn't sure if she should go or not.

This fine lady and others in the secretarial pool started in on me with what they knew or thought they knew about me, and my life's history. They started saying that I was just a party animal, a big drinker, a womanizer, a "good time Charlie", although a nice fellow employee. I was not someone to get involved with.

These ladies even told how I had dated and married a lady that used to work in the office, and that it had ended tragically in a bad divorce. They said also how I had married another lady who was a nurse, and how that too ended badly in divorce. They told her how I had dated up to three ladies at the same time. They thought I was a jerk when it came to women and having them in my life. NICE LADIES DO YOU THINK?

Wendy was totally shocked and said *"thank you"* to the ladies for their heads-up about me. It had helped with her decision. When I approached Wendy and asked if she had decided on a coffee or drink get-together after work, she just smiled and said *"I don't think so. I have heard some interesting comments about you, so I don't think it is a good idea".*

I told her that I knew where she had gotten her information and said *"In my defence, these are theories. The ladies don't know the whole story or the honest truth. Please let me explain myself".*

Wendy commented that I seemed genuine in my expression of my innocence and wanted to separate truth from lies. She would sincerely like to hear the truth, if I was going to be honest.

Wendy was a smart lady, and said that if I really wanted to talk, then she would meet me at Springbank Park by the main entrance where we could walk and talk. She added from that initial meeting she would then decide where things would go from there. We could meet right after work, since she had some free time that day.

I was very pleased with her statement, and relished the chance to iron out the false stories about me in the office gossip and to actually spend time with her. I was thrilled to be one-on-one with Wendy, just to be strolling along with simple conversation, in my attempt to build confidence and trust with her, and to be allowed an opportunity to explain myself. It was indeed a very special moment in my life.

In my excitement, I couldn't wait for the end of the day. I looked with anticipation for the time I would spend with Wendy and to hopefully win her over. The end of the day seemed far away, and the hands on the clock seemed motionless. I was like a child waiting for the official nod from a parent that it was alright to open a present. This was a new feeling for me, to be experiencing the waiting, the excitement, and unknown events looming on the horizon.

Everything was such an exhilaration of emotions inside me. The day's end finally arrived and I was hastily going to my car to start the drive to Springbank Park. I am not sure if I came to a full stop at all the lights and signs on my route, because the trip there was a bit of a blur. My mind was trying to organize my words and thoughts for my meeting with Wendy. Obviously, I had arrived first and there was no sign of her car coming down the roadway.

I waited several minutes not sure how much time had passed since I hadn't even looked at my watch. My mind was still rehearsing several opening lines to use once Wendy arrived. I was pacing up and down, like an expectant father and finally I saw Wendy's car approaching. Shortly after, she was parked and walking towards me.

Immediately, Wendy started to apologize for taking so long to arrive because she hadn't realized how little gas she had. It was mandatory she get some fuel or run out. These were her only two choices. I told her that it was not a problem. I was in no particular hurry to go home. In reality, I had all the time in the world. I had nothing to go home for anyway.

I expressed how happy I was with her decision to give me a chance to explain myself. Wendy said *"I believe there are two sides to every story, the truth and the lie. But I am here for the truth"*. I lost my whole train of thought when Wendy said that. She started walking and a few seconds later I realized she was in motion. I had to quickly get into step in order to catch up to her. We walked a long distance in entire silence. She waited for me to begin and I was trying to find the right words to start.

Finally, Wendy said *"I thought you were going to open up with the truth about your life on our walk. Have you changed your mind"?* I was totally caught off guard with this comment. Finally, I said that I was confused about where to begin. I told her it was indeed my intent to tell the truth; but could she just ask me some questions to help me see what she really wanted to know. Then I repeated myself and said again that I would give her honest answers to her questions because I had nothing to hide.

Wendy just laughed a kind laugh, and said *"I think I have already just learned something about you"*. I guess I must have looked bewildered as she continued, *"You seem shy, and nothing like the mover that I was told you were"*. I just smiled and then nodded a "yes" to her comment. This seemed to break the ice for me and a comfort zone had been established and the words started to flow. I became totally relaxed and my life history was starting to reveal itself. I felt very comfortable in this lady's company and she made me feel at ease with the kind way she was asking me personal questions.

She was asking and I was not in any way, shape or form, hiding the truth. I would add more information than she seemed to be asking. I was trying to establish honesty, integrity and truthfulness, in an attempt to gain her confidence and trust. I wanted to show my serious intention about wanting to spend time with her.

I told her that first, that I wanted to be a good friend to her. Then hopefully, I wanted to move into a relationship. Slow and easy was my approach for both of us. I felt a strong immediate bond of commitment, and an even stronger desire to spend the rest of my life with this lady. These comments were never expressed to Wendy at this time; but my mind and heart had totally been taken.

This totally absorbing feeling was now controlling my life and the pathway that I so wanted. It was not like any other feeling that I had ever had for any other woman. This feeling reminded me of the time I was totally lost in the fantasy world with my grade one teacher, and how I had blocked out the rest of the world just to look in awe at my "first love". This lady teacher's love I could never have, but nonetheless, she had stolen my heart from the very first moment that I had seen her.

This was the same parallel feeling I was now experiencing with Wendy. I was totally under her spell and wanted nothing else but to be in her world. Hopefully she would allow me to become involved in her life, and for us to build a commitment for our remaining time on this earth. This walk was so enjoyable and even though it was a "seek and find question period" it wasn't that kind of interrogation. It was just like two normal people trying to uncover each other's personalities.

Each of us was trying to learn about each other . . . our likes and dislikes, and trying to sense a connection to one another. Wendy did not know this, but I had already felt a strong bond and could only hope that she would find one for me and grant me more time to spend with her.

Wendy finally stopped walking and said *"I think you have cleared the air about any misconceptions that I may have had about you. Thank you for your honesty"*. I replied *"I promised the truth, and that is what I have delivered"*. She just smiled and said *"We had better start heading back to our cars and get homeward bound. It's getting late and I still have supper to prepare at home"*.

As we walked back, we both retreated to a world of silence, and it wasn't until we reached our cars, that I realized that I had better see if I had "passed the test". Hopefully I could spend more time in her company.

I said *"Could we go for another walk and talk with each other soon? Maybe later in the week"?* Wendy smiled and said *"I would like to do that and will let you know when it can be arranged"*. I smiled in acknowledgement and told her I was totally flexible with my time, so it would be at her convenience. We arrived at our cars, waved a friendly goodbye to one another and we were off in different directions.

It was Friday of that week that Wendy said *"How about Saturday afternoon for another walk in Springbank Park, around 2 p. m. at the same location as before"?* I replied to her *"I will be there with bells on"* and she just laughed and walked away. We had said earlier to each other in our first walk that we would keep a low profile about us going for a walk together, in order not to be the topic of conversation at the ladies' coffee break.

We had both been of the opinion that this was a very good decision, based on the way things were often blown out of proportion by this group. I could hardly wait till Saturday to come when I would have that connection with Wendy. I arrived at the meeting spot early to wait for her. I was still nervous and my pacing back and forth must have been watched by many people. But I was not aware of it until Wendy arrived and she said *"You look nervous, like someone who is about to go for a job interview"*.

We both just laughed aloud and I made light of it by saying, *"How perceptive of you to notice"*. She was already in motion at this point and my comment fell on deaf ears. Wendy was already heading into the park and we started off with small talk about her thoughts of the people in the work place, the job she was doing in the office, the office politics, and so on.

Then it got back to a more serious tone about the two of us. I told Wendy that I had told my mother about my meeting her for a walk today, and that she was pleased that I had a new friend. My mother had suggested that I ask about her family. My mother thought she already knew them. She told me that she was pretty sure that they had lived just a few homes away from my grandmother's house on Maple Street in St. Thomas.

When my parents were first married and after my sister and I were born, we all lived with my grandmother for 5 years, in order to save up money to buy their own home. She was pretty sure that Wendy and her sister Emily had asked to take me for a buggy ride when I was a baby. She also stated that the girls were only about 5 and 7 at the time and that in hindsight, she should not have let them take me for the buggy ride.

Mom said when the girls brought me back to her, they told her when they dropped me, my head was cut badly and I probably required stitches. My poor mother was in a state of shock and both the girls were crying. Mom said *"I'm sure you two will have a good laugh over that story, and thank God you had a thick skull"*. At the time Mom said that it was not funny. But all these years later one can now reminisce what indeed a small world it had turned out to be. Who would have thought it possible?

As I told Wendy this story, I could see her jaw slowly drop in disbelief and bewilderment. She could not believe the story and was totally taken aback. Wendy said *"I cannot believe that was you then. Now all these years later you are telling me this story. It's like fate put us back together on the same path in life. How amazing!"*

At this point I opened up and told her that I sincerely wanted to pursue a relationship with her, and about my feelings that I already had for her. How strange, and yet how comfortable I felt, expressing my feelings. I was also hopeful that she would give both of us time to explore our feelings. I was not rushing her for a decision, but merely letting her know about my desire for more walks, more talks, and wanting the time to move slowly and hopefully into a committed relationship.

I was not looking for a quick romance. I was in for the long haul, looking for a bond, for happiness, and for a soul-mate for the rest of my life. I hoped her desires were in that direction too. At this point,

Wendy grabbed my hand and we just continued walking in silence. As we were walking a poem came to me from my heart, and I wish to share it now with you.

MY SPIRIT IS ON HIGH

The touch of your soft warm hand;
Its closeness it brought me to you.
The smile that glowed from your face
Made me fall in love with you more.
My silent spirit now awakened,
And my heart was all aglow,
As you became a part of my life
And I would never let you go,
We had now been bonded together
As happiness became part of us.
Love was there for us to share
To pledge our love and life together
And never to break the seal.
Your world was now a part of mine.
My world was now with you.
Our body spirits both on high;
Our lives were born renewed.
For now we had found each other
With the true meaning for love and life;
Its pathway set for us to follow
Forever to stroll that way;
To walk hand in hand forever
Wherever life may lead us,
What ever strife may greet us.
Our love for one another
Would always see us through.

Wendy and I continued strolling along lost in our own thoughts, and finally I said to her *"A penny for your thoughts"*. Wendy said *"I was just thinking again about what the ladies in the office had said about you and how wrong they were and how very little they actually know about you"*.

I just smiled and then stated *"I'm glad you could see through them and their gossip, and I am so glad you gave me a chance to explain myself"*. At this point I pulled Wendy close to me and gave her gentle, warm, loving kiss and she replied in kind. We both knew what we had found in each other was a real commitment, a strong bond of connection and a longing for a life's partner had finally been realized with one another.

I wrapped my arms around Wendy and was drawn into an even closer connection to this lady with this simple act. I asked Wendy if she had any plans for supper, or for the balance of the evening. Wendy replied that she did not and would love to have supper with me, *"but let's continue enjoying our walk and this beautiful day"*.

It was as if my life was now beginning. Being connected to someone with the simple act of holding her hand, I was truly alive and very aware of nature's beauty. In fact for me, I was now looking at the whole world with a completely new interest, and awareness, a world I had not been involved in, but merely just existing in.

Wendy finally said to me, *"I do not even know what kind of foods you like. Maybe on our walk back to the cars, we could talk about that"?* I told Wendy about my likes and dislikes in foods and she told me about hers too. We finally decided we had some mutual likes about food to enjoy for supper that evening.

I was pleased to learn that Wendy was very down to earth in both dress, in places to eat and flexible in the dinner hour as well. She finally said she knew of a Kelsey's restaurant nearby and off we went in that direction. We were surprised at the time of day and how long we had been walking and talking.

Time seemed so insignificant; but in reality it was nearly 6:00 p.m. and four hours had already passed. We arrived at Kelsey's which was a bar/restaurant establishment; but being the prime dinner hour, we had to go to the bar area and wait for a table to become available.

Here too I learned that Wendy liked beer and she ordered. I responded with *"Crown Royal and water for me."* Wendy said *"Well now I know something new about you I didn't know before. You obviously do not like beer"*. I replied *"No I don't, and if you would like a mixed drink rather than a beer, please feel to change your drink order"*. Then I said *"I'm not worried about the cost of your drink or your meal so please order what you really wish, rather than something that is low cost, just to please me."*

Wendy said *"Thank you for clearing that up, because I didn't want to be an expensive dinner date for you"*.

I told Wendy that the cost was not a concern and would prefer if she would be herself now, just as she had been earlier in the day. It was going on 8:30 p.m. when we were leaving the restaurant and Wendy asked if I would like to follow her home, and to come in for tea. I followed her home to an apartment building on Wonderland Road, and thought how close she was to me. I think I found the last parking space in the apartment complex and soon joined her at the entrance.

She lived on the ground floor in a surprisingly large two bedroom apartment with her son Brent. When we walked into the apartment, Brent was there with a couple of his friends watching a baseball game on TV. Wendy introduced me to her son and his friends; then got busy making us two cups of herbal tea, a new flavour she had discovered and was anxious to try out.

One of the boys said *"How about tea for us as well"?* Wendy responded with *"Since when did you boys start liking herbal tea? But help yourself. I'm not your mother"*. The boys all laughed, and said *"Ok Mom"*, and continued watching the TV. I looked at Wendy and she just laughed back at them, and I then discovered her sense of humour, and the strong bond she had with her son and his friends. The boys were going fishing early the next day so their evening soon broke up.

Now it was just Wendy and I there alone. Wendy told me that she had two daughters that lived elsewhere in the city and that Brent was the last one to leave the nest. We spent time looking through her family photo album and enjoying each other's company. Because it was getting late, I told Wendy that I had a wonderful day with her; in fact it was the best day I had had in a long time. But now I had to go.

I asked her if I could call or see her tomorrow, and she said that Sunday was her cleaning and laundry day. But she would love to talk with me later in the day. A sweet, light kiss at the doorway good night, and I was off home. After my break up with Erin, I had bought a large two storey home, complete with a 20x40 in-ground pool. In God's name I do not know why, but that is what I had purchased.

In reality, it was too large a home for a single person. But it caught my eye in the real estate market. I talked with Wendy that Sunday evening and asked how her day had gone, and she asked the same of me.

In our discussion, Wendy finally said *"Where do you live?"* We had not talked about that yet. I told her she would probably not believe me; but I was only fifteen minutes from where she lived. I told her how surprised I was once I knew where she lived how close we really were.

We both had a good laugh and I invited her over for a swim the next weekend or sooner if she wished. Wendy said *"You have a pool as well?"* I told her how big it was and she was shocked and said *"Oh my God, that is huge, like a small pond".* I do not know why but the time seemed to be on fast forward, and all too soon it was time to say goodnight. I looked forward to seeing her at work the next day.

We both kept a low profile in the office to avoid being the topic of office gossip, but because we knew each other's phone extensions, we would call one another and chat briefly. Our Monday morning chat surprised me when Wendy said she would like to come over to see my home and have that swim this coming weekend. I asked Wendy if she would trust me to barbeque a dinner after the swim. She said *"It will give me a chance to see what kind of a chef you are"* and she said she was looking forward to it.

We continued with brief talks on the office phone system and had longer conversations at night on our private home phones throughout the week. We wanted to know so much about one another that our questions seemed endless. One question and answer would always lead to another from either of us. Our desire was to know all that there was to know about each other on an honest basis. We didn't want to listen to any of the "office gossip".

It was as though we were young teenagers just starting to date and wanting to know it all. However unlike teenagers our questions were serious. We were building something concrete, much like a couple who had been married for years and knew each other inside and out.

We wanted NO SECRETS, NO SURPRISES and NO UNKNOWNS, to exist between us . . . just the truth. We wanted to be "an open book" to one another. Neither of us could contain ourselves for the upcoming weekend and spending quality time together. Saturday afternoon finally had arrived; I was like a boy going on his first date, busily moving items from here to there and back again.

I was trying so desperately to make a good impression, to make everything appear to be in its right place. I wanted things to look "normal". I was also constantly looking at the clock and waiting for the doorbell to ring. I walked back and forth in anticipation. I do not know for the life of me, why I was so nervous.

But this was the first time Wendy would be in my home and I wanted everything to look great and not appear like I lived like a slob and that I had a good sense of home decorating. Wendy was finally ringing the bell and as I opened the door, I reached up to give her a welcoming hug. Wendy was pleased with the hug and responded that she was happy to see me as well.

I think that she was momentarily a little surprised by my greeting; but took it as a simple "*happy to see you*", with no sexual overtones and she calmed down. I asked her if she would like to see through my home before our swim and she said she would like the grand tour. There was plenty of house to show her, so we started in the finished basement, then went on through the ground floor, and finally to the second floor with the four bedrooms and two baths.

Wendy exclaimed "*What in God's name possessed you to buy such a large home for yourself? Are you nuts*"? She then broke into laughter and said "*I wish we had been together before you bought this home. I would have liked to have helped you find one more reasonably sized, that would not have required so much decorating*". I told her that I wished we had been together as well, before I bought this home. It would have been a lot more fun looking at different homes together and getting a woman's perspective on the whole issue.

I said to Wendy "*Would you like to help me decorate this home to make it into our home*"? She was speechless at this point and when she spoke, she said "*Do I understand you correctly? You want my son and me to move in here together with you*". I said "*Wendy, you know my true feelings for you, and yes I honestly do want you and your son to live with me*". Wendy said "*This all seems so sudden. Our relationship is moving so fast. I just can't believe myself. Am I in a dream or is this truly reality*"?

I told Wendy that my heart, my soul, my very being, wanted nothing more than having her in my life. When everything is just so right, then you have to follow your heart and not risk losing something so special. I repeated myself saying that my heart's desire was to have her with me, for the rest of my life.

At this point, Wendy just sat down in the chair in the family room and said she felt like her head was spinning. I leaned over her and kissed her first softly on the neck, then on her cheek. As she turned towards me, I placed a passionate, loving kiss to her lips. My arms went around her in a secure hug showing my total desire to have her in my life and in OUR home.

Wendy then stated *"I feel safe, secure, and do feel a loving bond to you Paul. How happy you have made me! Now my life also is complete with you in it"*. Wendy and I finally got to have our swim and enjoyed frolicking in the pool, playing kid's games, doing "cannon balls" off the diving board and swimming under water to one another, pulling one another under the water for brief kisses.

Finally we were just standing there side by side, holding hands, talking, hugging. In short we were just enjoying the moment together, and our bond to one another. Wendy finally said *"Hey chef, are you going to feed me or not"?* I hopped out of the pool and started the barbeque, and replied *"Your wish is my command"* and we both just laughed. I told Wendy to just rest in the sunlight or to go under the umbrella and that I would get the hamburgers on the grill.

I had purchased a variety of salads and even a dessert to make this my first meal I prepared for Wendy. I wanted it to be special and I also wanted to show that I was a good "boy scout" always being prepared. After dinner we both returned to sit beside the pool to enjoy the evening and each other's company. It was getting darker, and Wendy surprised me with *"Do you want to go skinny dipping"?* I told her I was game if she was, and with that the clothing came off and I could see Wendy's lovely body silhouetted by the moonlight as she slipped into the water.

I was quickly in there beside her, kissing her passionately, and our hands roamed each other's bodies. I was enjoying the tingling touch responses of Wendy's body. As quickly as it had begun, Wendy said *"I am sorry for leading you on. I'm not ready yet in our relationship to make love to you"*.

Wendy got out of the pool, grabbing a towel and her clothing and was off into the house. I was momentarily stunned and just stood there in the pool wondering what had happened. What was wrong with me? What had I done that I shouldn't have? Was everything now falling apart in this new relationship? I was totally confused. What should I do now?

I left the pool, grabbed my clothes and towel off the chair and went into the house. I needed to confront Wendy about what had just happened. At this point, she was already dressed. I asked her to wait till

I got dressed, so we could talk. Wendy said she would wait because she also wanted to clear the air about what was going on in her head.

As I walked back into the room, Wendy said *"I'm sorry for getting you so excited. I thought I was really ready to make love with you; but I didn't want you to think I was easy when it came to sex"*. Wendy said she was replaying the comments from the ladies at work in her mind; that I was just a "good time Charlie" and she had her doubts about those comments.

She thought that I was just playing her to get sex. Was I truly sincere about wanting her in my life? These questions were playing havoc within her, so she had to stop and re-evaluate everything we had said to be totally sure that this was genuine. She did not want to get hurt again by any man!

I walked over to Wendy, put my arms around her, wiped the tears from her cheek, and said *"My beautiful lady, I want you desperately in my life, for the rest of my life. I am not just looking to have sex with you. I would be telling a lie if I said that I don't want sex, because I'm looking forward to it. But I am willing to wait till you are comfortable with me before we go there"*.

Wendy said *"I am so sorry"*, and started to hug me tightly. She said *"Thank you for understanding and not putting pressure on me"*. I walked her to the front door, kissed her long and passionately, told her again that I was always here for her. I was not going anywhere, and that there was not going to be any pressure. I would move at her pace. I loved her, and that I wanted her in my life from now on. One more good night kiss and she was off home.

When Sunday morning arrived, I heard the phone ringing. As I listened I heard Wendy say *"Good morning Paul. Thank you for a great day yesterday and for understanding. Thank you for wanting to be a part of my life"*. I told her how nice it was to start the day hearing her voice and that I enjoyed her company too. I wanted her to know that she could always trust me. She told me that she hadn't slept very much last night and she did a lot of thinking over a lot the comments she had heard, including mine.

She looked into her heart to search her true feelings for me. She realized that I was indeed what she wanted in her life and her feelings for me were very strong. I replied, *"I love you very much and you are very special to me, and that you will remain that way for the rest of my life"*. She said *"I want to come over. Is that alright?"* Jokingly, I said *"What about your housework"*? I then quickly added that I was hoping she would come over because I wanted to give her a hug and a kiss.

Wendy was soon at my door, and as promised I hugged her and kissed her and this time she was happy with my greeting. We spent the rest of the day just talking, laying on the couch, holding one another, enjoying the time together, totally unaware of the time passing. We were totally lost in one another. How wonderful the day was because now Wendy had a totally firm grip on her feelings and my feelings too. She was totally comfortable with everything. LOVE WAS TRULY ALIVE WITHIN BOTH OF US.

Wendy and I talked about our future together and she said that one of her daughter's birthdays was coming this week. *"I guess it's time for you to come to my apartment for a birthday dinner and meet the rest of my family"*. Then she said *"They will probably want to give you the third degree"*. At this point she laughed, and added, *"They already know all about you"*. I told Wendy that I would love to meet her other two children, and it might be interesting to see what kind of a cook she was. *"Just kidding"* I said.

Next Saturday was the night for the birthday dinner. So I took over a couple of bottles of wine and a birthday card with some money in it for the occasion. Upon arrival I gave Wendy a kiss at the doorway, and was surprised as all three children stood there with their mouths open. They also were part of the greeting committee. She thanked me for the wine, and then introduced me to her two daughters, Laura, and Jennifer, and I already knew Brent.

Wendy said *"Great timing, since supper is going to be a little earlier than planned. I put the food in the oven too soon"*. I was told it was Laura's birthday so I offered her the card. I wanted to make a good first impression to everyone. Wendy had made a birthday cake, and we all sang happy birthday to Laura. Even she blushed with happiness, and it was an enjoyable time for everyone.

Wendy said we could open the wine later if I was up to playing a board game with them. It seemed I had just become a member of her family. Wendy's kids and I hit it off right from the start, and at this point my heart was totally content. Life seemed RICH and FULL and all was right in my world. From this point on, life with Wendy seemed very happy, tranquil and positive.

We discussed having a Thanksgiving Dinner with her children, and to finally meet my parents. I thought it would be an appropriate time to do so. All the plans were set. It was a great time working in the kitchen with Wendy and her daughters. It seemed a "family unit" had been formed. My parents finally arrived to a very busy household. All of Wendy's kids had brought dates to join in the festivities. My parents were in total amazement with all the loud voices; but I knew from their smiles, they were totally pleased with everything.

I introduced them to Wendy, her kids, and their dates, and as I was doing so, my happiness bubbled over. For the very first in my life time, it was a proud moment to be introducing my new family. What a wonderful Thanksgiving Day! All the people I loved were together under one roof. I couldn't be any happier than at that moment.

As my parents were leaving, my mother was giving me a goodbye kiss said *"I have never seen you so happy. You have a special lady. Don't lose her!"* I told Mom, *"She is my life now, and I have no intention of losing her and the happiness she was bringing into my life!"* Mom gave me another hug and kiss. Then she said, *"I'm very happy for you Paul. It does my heart good to finally see you so happy".* Clean up after dinner went extremely well as many hands made light work. Soon we were all sitting in the family room, digesting the large meal, having some easy conversation, and sipping some wine. As Wendy's kids and dates were leaving, we stood at the doorway like the real parents, and said our good nights. Wendy said as we re-entered the family room, *" Thank you for having all of us together in your home. It would have been very crowded in my apartment for all of us."* I told her *"Wendy, this is now going to be your home . . . not just mine, and of course your kids are always welcome anytime to our home".* Wendy kissed me passionately and said *"I love you Paul. You are special and have made me very happy. I am looking forward to spending the rest of my life with you".*

From that very moment, I knew we were soul-mates; we could face anything and conquer it together. We were one with each other. Our love bond was now complete.

Now we were the occasional topic of conversation in the office. But this time it was not gossip. Rather, people noticed a change in me, in my mood, my total personality. It was always positive and nobody saw any swing in my moods. Why would there be? My happiness was there . . . literally and figuratively in the office and contentment filled my mind. I thought everyone in the office must be aware of my love for this lady, unless they were blind and dumb.

Good news! Wendy was offered a permanent position and it seemed that we could now build our lives together since she was assured of a full-time position. She was a very independent lady, and wouldn't let anyone be her "keeper"; she wanted to feel she was able to contribute to our lives with her own money and she needed that security.

It was now getting close to Christmas, and I discovered it was Wendy's favourite and happiest time of the year. She asked if she could come over and help me decorate the Christmas tree. Since I am not really into decorating, I was very pleased. Wendy came over that Friday night and we ordered in a pizza, to have a quick supper before getting into decorating.

I could instantly see the glow in Wendy's face as she went about decorating the tree. It was like watching an artist at work on his canvas. I handed her this and that decoration, and she looked for just the right spot to place it. What a wonderful piece of artwork was been created, one worthy of putting on a Hallmark card! I watched in amazement. Wendy asked me to plug in the cord to see its beauty. As I stood up, Wendy stood beside me and my arm went around her. I was so filled with the SPIRIT OF CHRISTMAS in that very instant. The total beauty before me was all consuming. It seemed as if the world was at peace; that love and joy surrounded us both.

I kissed Wendy's cheek, and as she turned our lips touched softly, and then our mouths opened and our hands started to roam over each other's bodies. My fingers started to fumble at the buttons on her blouse; her hands were tugging at my belt, trying to take my pants off. We were lying there nude, entwined with each other. The bells, whistles, and sirens were all going off at the same time, as we headed for the climax of ecstasy. Both our bodies were reaching for that moment of climax.

Finally, we both lay in a sweaty pool; our faces still aglow; our arms still tightly wrapped around one another. We were both speechless, but realized that we had given the greatest Christmas gift of all to each other.

A LOVE FOR EACH OTHER; A TOTAL COMMITMENT TO LIFE TOGETHER; A UNION OF OUR SPIRITS FOR LIFE HAD BEEN WELDED TOGETHER. Sharing our Love under the

Christmas tree seemed the complete expression of God's love for both of us.

Wendy said *"We are now one, my love; my life I give to you"*. I responded to Wendy *"We are now one, my love; my life I give to you"*.

It was as though we had just signed a contract before God and the world, that we were now a life-time couple, and we would face life together, forever.

Once again, we had her children, their dates, and my parents for a Christmas dinner. We enjoyed the meal preparation together, along with the love and warmth of a family Christmas. Wendy and I looked lovingly at each other across the table. I raised my wine glass and said *"To all a merry Christmas, and thank you for coming to make this occasion so special. Thank you for coming into my life. May you all find joy in your lives, love in your hearts and peace in your souls. That is what this Special Lady . . . your mother . . . has given to me, and I wish the same to everyone gathered here"*.

This had been the most enjoyable Christmas of my whole life. I had found my true love; I had my family here, as well as my new family. I could not have wished for one single other thing in my life. My treasure chest was brimming over with all that I ever wanted out of life.

From this point on, life with Wendy was filled with daily, happy memories. We had found what both of us had been searching for in our lives. We were totally willing to give ourselves to totally sharing happiness with each other. Life was indeed rich and full as we settled into a world of contentment and happiness with one another.

It was now an unbelievably smooth ride in life with Wendy by my side. When life threw speed bumps my way or hers, we had each other as a sounding board and we resolved the problem. Either one of us always smoothed out the bumps and got us back to clear sailing.

Time was marching on but it didn't alter our feelings for one another and our love for one another was always expressed in many different forms. Everyone could plainly see that this bond we shared was unshakeable and was forever constant.

I was now coming up to my 50th birthday and wondered what my lady had up her sleeve. Wendy arranged for 50 pink pigs and a happy birthday sign to be placed on our front lawn. When I was coming for my morning coffee, she led me to the front door saying that there was something wrong outside that I had to see. You could have knocked me down with a feather when I opened the door. The happiness it brought me was indescribable.

But my Wendy was not quite done. When I arrived at work, there were balloons above and around my desk. My fellow employees had decorated it, and a birthday cake complete with candles was sitting on my desk. Some of the employees close by were singing "happy birthday" as I approached my desk. The rest of the office staff was watching these antics.

My lady, my Wendy, had given me a gift far beyond my wildest dreams. I had never received anything in my lifetime that could come close to match this celebration. I could hardly hold back my tears. How blessed I was with the love from this woman and the joy she brought to my life. To say turning 50 was the thrill of my life would be an understatement and it will be etched in my mind for my remaining years on this earth.

Wendy had made this occasion not only very special for me; but it was one that she totally shared in and one that the both of us could share for the rest of our lives.

I now had only six months of working time before I retired. Here too, this lady was making plans to have this memory one we could share, as well as being a big part of it. Wendy had looked into an 18-day European Tour for us to share and to mark the retirement day permanently in my mind. I was totally amazed, thrilled, and bewildered at how she had done all the pre-preparation work without me knowing or seeing pamphlets laying around the house.

Once Wendy had a firm handle on the trip we would be taking, she announced its schedule, the time and cost. I was elated with her plans, and thought how special was the love this woman gave me and how lucky I was to have her in my life. Wendy wanted only to see me happy and knew I was a little uptight about retirement. Consequently, this was the plan to have these memories together for the rest of our lives and look at retirement with different eyes.

We put the wheels in motion, got our passports, went to the travel agency about the tour package, signed the contracts, put down the deposit and even got various currencies for the different countries we would be seeing. We went out and bought new suitcases for each other; checked our wardrobe and went to the doctor for the necessary travel medication. All this organization seemed like a job in itself; but both Wendy and I liked all the preparation work firmly in place, so things would go smoothly.

Retirement day was soon upon me, it was such a strange feeling. I knew I would be walking out the doors for the very last time, and that the people I worked with for so many years would not likely be present in my life again. In fact I would soon be forgotten by them. I actually had tears in my eyes and my life seemed different. I shook different people's hands as I walked to the door and realized that this part of my life was now finished. It gave me a weird feeling, and that somehow this day was like a funeral. It was a very weird feeling; but I guess one, that other retirees may also go through.

That night Wendy sensed my uneasiness, possibly a mild depression and was quickly by my side. She put her arms around me, touched soft kisses to my cheek, and she said *"You have only closed one chapter of your working life; you still have many chapters of me in your life, as well as many chapters of memories to build with me"*. This seemed to have done the trick, and I realized she was totally right. My life was not over. It was like being reborn. A new life and a new lifestyle were now opening for me to venture into. What new possibility would be presented?

I THANK GOD FOR WENDY AND HER WISDOM, STRENGTH, AND HER LOVE AT THIS STAGE OF MY LIFE. WITHOUT HER, WHO KNOWS WHAT MY MENTAL STATE WOULD HAVE BEEN?

Wendy still had a few years of work to go since she had started here much later than I and would still have to build up a good retirement fund for herself. We went on that European Tour which included England, Belgium, Germany, Holland, France and Switzerland. What a fantastic time we had with new cultures, sites, foods, and savouring memories we were sharing. These memories would allow us to recall and share with one another down the road of our life about our first "real" holiday together. What a way to celebrate retirement and to have a special lady to share each of the experiences with, made it all that much more memorable and meaningful.

To say that Wendy was the best gift that God had ever given me would be an understatement. With her in my life, I was able to experience life in all its glory. Life was overflowing with happiness and every fibre of my being was totally stimulated, enjoying all that was being sent my way.

As they say, all good things finally come to an end. So it was with our vacation. After most vacations there is always a little letdown. Life as you knew it was going to resume its normal routine. As Wendy went out the door for work, I gave her a small kiss and said *"Have a nice day!"* I was left behind feeling a little lost. Normally I too would be heading off to work.

What in God's name do I do with myself all day? I had not done any planning for this day in my life. I had no hobbies, no real outside interests, and most of my friends were still working. Was I going to be a house mother? I made the bed, did up the few dishes, and started some laundry. But what now?

I had to plan dinner of course but what did I know about cooking? Well, since I had all the time in the world, I had better learn. If I was on my own, I could have made Kraft dinner; but I wanted to do something special for my first meal for Wendy. I started reading instructions on boxes and cans. Then realized like work, I had to have a plan. What am I having first? Then I could see about adding the extras. This was a totally new world to me; but even though it was a challenge, I was up to the task.

I decided to have a chicken dinner for Wendy's arrival home. I got out the chicken to thaw; made Jello and peeled potatoes and carrots. I went to the grocery store and bought cheese, different types of pickles, stove top stuffing, dinner rolls, and even bought a cake for dessert. I also picked up a dozen roses for the centre piece on the table.

I was starting to be amazed at how much work was involved in preparing a meal and the amount of time involved. Back at home it was time to get the chicken in the oven; set the table; arrange the flowers, and wait for the time to start the vegetables. Then I made up the cheese and pickle trays, and realized it was time for a break . . . to mellow out and have a drink of Crown Royal. I decided it was well deserved.

I turned on the TV and busied myself surfing all the channels to find something to watch other than soap operas. At the office, we all used to joke about afternoon soap operas. I still remember some of the guys in the office telling stories about how their wives became so connected to these soaps. It was just as though it was a part of their everyday existence. It was almost an essential part in their lives and they couldn't stand to miss what was happening.

I eventually found a discovery channel dealing with wild life in Africa and settled in to enjoy the scenery and the different species of animals. After the show finished, I started the vegetables cooking; even got a bottle of wine chilled for our dinner.

When Wendy arrived home, I greeted her with a kiss at the door and she said *"I could get used to this kind of welcome home"*, as she wandered into the kitchen following the fragrant smell of the food on the stove for dinner. I was pleased that her curiosity had led her into the kitchen as it was a pleasant smell and not one of food burning. I was pleased about that and that panic had not overtaken her.

Wendy exclaimed *"Oh my God . . . the roses; the table is set; everything smells delightful. I think I will keep you"*. I open the chilled wine and gave us both a glass and told her to sit down and tell me of her day, along with the daily gossip. She was totally blown away with the meal and told me this was like "Sunday" dinner and must have taken me all day to prepare. I told her that I wanted to surprise her and make her happy with my first attempt at a full meal.

Wendy said *"Paul you have outdone yourself and yes you have made me very happy with all your efforts and the love you put into making everything so special"*. Then she said *"You know just having the table set and a simple meal in the future would be great. We can't eat like this all the time, or we will be big as houses in no time"*. I told Wendy that this was all new to me, but thanked her for the "heads-up" in the meal preparation, but still I wondered what I was going to do with all my free time

I went to a nearby nursing home because Wendy had said suggested that I consider doing some volunteer work. There are always many people who need assistance. I was surprised at how quickly they had me on staff. Wendy was correct. Indeed, there was a large need for helping hands. I was putting in a lot of hours, upwards of 40 hours a week, and told the lady who had brought me on board about this.

She just said *"There are so many people who need help and so too few to help out that you are indeed a Godsend"*. I told her that I was feeling a little guilty, that I must be taking a job from somebody else, because of the number of hours she had me working. The lady just responded that there was no money to hire extra staff. I guess it was a little guilt trip on my part for even questioning the amount of time I was working.

There were indeed a lot of big men living in the home that needed my help because a lot of the ladies found it difficult to handle taking them around. I was making a lot of people's lives a little easier, so I was often told. I worked as a volunteer for nearly a year at this nursing home; but I was still feeling that they were taking advantage of me. Finally I had enough, and gave in my notice.

I told Wendy what I had decided and she was in agreement; but told me she did not want to interfere and wanted me to decide what was best for me. Then she said *"Well what are you going to try next to do with all your free time"?* I told her I had no real hobbies that I thought I might look for a job. Wendy just smiled and said *"Whatever makes you happy; although I really have been missing all your help in the kitchen".* It was true. All the hours I had been putting in at the nursing home meant that usually Wendy was home before me and had to start meal preparation. I would usually assist wherever I could when I got home and was sure to do all the after dinner cleanup, so that Wendy could have some free time.

I found a job with a security company and much to my surprise the hours of work were totally strange to me. I could not believe that people actually worked those hours. I had never known about this. Although in hindsight, I knew my parents had both worked them. I was used to an 8 to 4 work day, not an 11 to 7 work day. This would be a totally new world to me and would require a major adjustment in my life as well as in Wendy's and our lifestyle together.

I did this "hobby job" for two years and finally came to my senses and said *"I don't need this job; so if you don't find me one with better working hours, I will have to give notice. I have no home life with Wendy".* The timing must have been just right because a position of a parking lot attendant at Fanshawe College became available. The hours of work were from 7:30 a.m.-1:30 p.m. with no weekends, no holidays and no summer employment.

This meant that when the kids were in school I worked, and when they were not present I did not have to work. How great is that? This seemed like the perfect hours for a "hobby job" so I accepted it. It was shortly thereafter, that Wendy's health started going downhill. I was soon taking her to x-ray appointments, doctor appointments, and specialist appointments. It was all in an attempt to find out how we could get to the root of her health issue.

Finally after trying a variety of medications and seeing a variety of specialists, that we discovered that my Wendy had CANCER. We cried in each other's arms. It was as though the wind had been ripped out of Wendy's sails and my heart had been torn from my body. The devastating news plunged us both into a state of despair with a total feeling of helplessness. How do we fight this disease? How do I not lose my Wendy?? I remembered at this moment a reality check if you will, that brought my feelings to the surface.

There are five things that you CANNOT recover in life.

1. THE STONE. . . . . after it is thrown, the effect is still felt
2. THE WORD . . . . after you have spoken it, you await its effect
3. THE OCCASION. . . . after it has been enjoyed, or even been missed
4. THE TIME . . . . after it's gone; it reminds you how precious it was
5. A PERSON . . . . after they die, you only have memories

These values and messages that I was recalling made me even sadder. I could not relish the thought of my SPECIAL LADY not being in my life.

Wendy was my pillar, my strength, my very root of life itself. Wendy and I made a pact that through thick or thin, we would always be by each other's side; to always love; always support and always guide each other through whatever happens; to fight and overcome this disease. We hoped that with our positive attitudes and combined strengths that it would prove to be enough to overcome all the obstacles.

At the early stages of this cancer, our lives didn't seem to be affected to any major degree, other than more frequent appointments to her regular doctor for medication changes. We were still enjoying life together. We were able to go out for meals or have friends in. Life was not throwing us any major curves . . . yet. Wendy and I were still able to have weekend trips alone or with friends. In fact Wendy was still able to go to work, at least initially. This however was short lived as she tired quickly and soon work itself was not an option.

All too soon the cancer clinic at the hospital was becoming like a "second home" to us. There were regular chemo and cancer doctor appointments and follow-ups to these appointments. An attempt with radiation treatments were thrown in for an added try to slow down the cancer; but to no avail. Wendy was mentally, a very strong woman, and kept a very positive attitude. This was a definite plus in the fight with cancer and the effects it was having on her body.

It was at this stage that Wendy needed home-care to help her with personal hygiene; to make her a light breakfast and lunch, and see to her medications. The home-care worker also did some light exercises with her, as well as changed her bedding and looking after the laundry. All this service was looked after by the cancer clinic. Because of its presence, Wendy insisted that I keep my "hobby job" as a parking lot attendant. Wendy stated that I needed an escape for own my "mental health" stability. She knew I would be home early afternoon and evenings to be with her.

I would come home from my job and the home care worker would be just leaving. I would sit on the side of Wendy's bed and share the events of each other's day. Then Wendy would then take a short nap. I would look into meal preparation and would then get Wendy up for supper and have the pleasure of her company to chat with during our meal and the balance of the evening.

On the weekends we would still have our outings with one another, although it was with the aid of a wheelchair, and the time spent out was on a reduced schedule. It was still wonderful to be out with her but she tired quickly, if she attempted to over-extend herself. Sometimes she believed she still could do all that she used to be able to do. That is not to say she didn't quite frequently push herself to the extreme. Before Wendy's sickness, she was a marathon shopper and she so loved to do this. Now it was more like possibly a two or three hour outing and she was all in, but her shoe laces, as the saying goes.

It was a reasonably normal life pattern, just on a shorter time table. But, Wendy still looked forward to these outings, and I was more than willing to make her happy. I was always very vigilant with her activities and the time she spent doing them, to try to make sure she didn't tire herself out to the ninth degree.

Time was quick-stepping along. Wendy's health was being more and more affected, and the trips to the hospital to get her chemo treatments was about all that she could handle in a day's outing. This would definitely affect our time and our personal outings together. However on a good day, Wendy was sure to tell me she wanted to go out for an hour or two. It was quite apparent that her health was sliding downhill. She had been fighting this cancer for almost four years, and I had watched her dying slowly, before my very eyes every day.

And this thought came to mind . . . MAY OUR FRIENDSHIP, LOVE, AND CONNECTION TO ONE ANOTHER, BE STRONG NOW AND WELL ON INTO ETERNITY.

My Wendy's love for me was so deep that she couldn't bear to leave me with all that was involved when it became necessary to prepare for a funeral. On one of her very last outings, she pushed her energy level to the very last ounce she could muster. She picked out the funeral home, her service, her guest signature register and even the thank you cards to be sent out. She selected the flowers that she wanted her children to give her, as well as those she wanted from me, along with the music she wanted played at the service.

Wendy wanted people to be touched by her "FAREWELL WORDS" and wanted people to know these were her last thoughts. She found a hallmark card that fit perfectly for the feelings she wanted expressed. Let me share them with you now.

> *HER VOICE STILL ECHOES;*
> *HER LIFE STILL INSPIRES;*
> *HER LIGHT STILL SHINES,*
> *AND ALWAYS WILL.*
> *I'M SO THANKFUL THAT I KNEW HER.*
> *SHE LIVES ON IN SO MANY HEARTS*
> *INCLUDING MINE.*
> *OUR LIVES ARE STILL CONNECTED-*
> *HEART TO HEART AND SOUL TO SOUL.*

Reading this, I am sure you can quickly begin to understand how SPECIAL this lady was and how blessed I was to have her in my life. She had a very "SPECIAL HEART" and we shared a very "SPECIAL LOVE".

What a comforting thought . . . what love, what a gift and what peace to be loved that much, that she wanted to spare me further pain from her death. This gift is beyond any words that I can imagine. I truly believe that this was my Wendy's final goal—to give me comfort and in my grief, to let me know that her spirit would be with me; that her love was forever—as mine is for her.

I honestly think that Wendy knew that her time to leave me was soon, because once she had accomplished all these preparations, it was as though her energy finally had now gone; her strength had been totally extinguished, and her ability to fight any longer was now void.

It was as though the final appointed hour for her existence was known only to her. She said to me *"IT'S TIME FOR ME TO LEAVE YOU, MY LOVE".*

Wendy lay in her bed, almost motionless, and I could sense death standing in the doorway, waiting to take her. I fought him off for twelve hours, holding her hands, holding back my tears, trying to be strong for my LADY. I spoke to Wendy about "our lives, our love and our life's journey together" as I watched her drift ever so slowly, into an even deeper sleep . . . and she was gone,

I thought my heart would tear itself from my chest and join her heart. But it had a strong purpose to remain "AS ONE HEART, FUNCTIONING FOR TWO BODIES". I take great comfort in knowing that I was blessed with such a love, and knew that Wendy was finally free from pain and was now at peace. I also knew that I now had a "SPECIAL ANGEL" who would continue to watch over me.

MISSING YOU IN MY LIFE

My life is very hollow
And full of despair.
I need you in my life
To give me warmth and laughter
As only you can do,
To make my world go from upside down
To right side up with you.

Now with Wendy gone, life as I knew it was a total shambles. There has to be a total re-adjustment in lifestyles and life's little habits. There is a distinct loss of someone to communicate with, to share everyday problems and happiness with . . . even to share more delicate or painful thoughts.

Everything is gone! The life preserver you had when you felt you were flailing in the sea of life is now gone. Your comfort zone is void; there are no loving arms to hold you and give you a sense of security and peace in your time of pain. You are now totally "on your own and feeling lost".

You now question your every decision, your strength of conviction, and your every purpose in life. Everything now seems like it happened so long ago.

You are now like a new-born baby . . . feeling helpless, needing direction, support and a gentle shove to take those first steps. Fear and uncertainty are always present and you are ever mindful of this "new life . . . alone".

I AM ALONE
I AM SCARED
I AM UNHAPPY
I AM UNLOVED

I'm not sure why I am here, or even if I want to be here. I am like a ship floating on life's ocean; not even sure where the currents are taking me.

IN MEMORY OF WENDY JANE McCARTHY

As you go through life's challenges
You'll have your ups and downs.
But when you find your soul-mate
The challenges will dissipate.
She is always there to cheer you up
And intervene on your behalf.
She's there at the end of the day
To make your life's circle last.
A rare jewel to say the least
She can always make you smile
And encourage you to do your best
This special girl of mine.

I cherish the time I had with her;
Her memories still live on.
Time continues to move forward;
Life seems an endless flow.
Separation still exists between us;
My heart still does not glow.
But I know the best is yet to come
When I am reunited with her.
Life's circle will then be complete
Further goodbyes will not exist.

For all eternity, they will remain in your heart and in your mind, and in your very soul. They will be a constant force to help you find yourself, your very purpose in life and will be your anchor in the troubled times. They will be with you till calm returns and you can continue to move forward in life.

My final tribute to my beautiful lady, my soul-mate, my anchor in life, as well as my comfort zone, is to leave you with a final poem I have created as an expression of my love and my loss.

MY LOVE IS FOREVER

I once was blessed with love;
The feeling of closeness to you.
You were my gift from God above
To have the whole day through.
Now my life is changed
No longer safe in my arms;
Your time has come to leave me
My sense of worth removed.
The void of closeness to you
Now fills my world completely.
I must now search my memories
For your love I surely need.
Rest now my love, my lady,
As my love will never die.

> *I know we'll be together.*
> *We will always live forever;*
> *Our minds will be connected*
> *Through all eternity.*

I am now: *Connecting to Grief*
            Coping with Grief
            Conquering Grief
            Continuing life without Grief

I am now in the Winter Season of my life, where I hope to find a partner, a best friend, someone to enjoy many happy moments and memories. I would still like to walk in sunshine on life's pathway to the final destination of being together here on earth as it comes to an end. But spirits are united for all eternity.

About the Author

I was born in the city of St. Thomas, which 62 years later, has a population of 33,000 people. It was very much smaller when I was growing up and it seemed that everyone knew everyone, as well as they knew what was happening in everyone else's life.

It is in this background setting, that I took my life's experiences for this book. I have tried to enlighten the reader about how "inept" I was in pursuing someone special in my life.

I am not trying to appear as the victim; but rather as someone who was struggling to follow in the footsteps of those who had the life skills I seemed to be lacking. My utopia was to find someone special to go together through life's ups and downs and build some very special memories.

One last item I want you to know is that I have written three other books that are totally to the "right" of this subject matter.

Now You Have Her . . . Now You Don't
This first book was written as a tribute to my wife who died in 2004.

That Single Moment
This book dealt with the emotions of losing a loved one and the healing process one goes through to "restart" life on your own.

Estate Planning & Executor's Guide
This workbook layout deals with the preparation and the organizing of your affairs before death and before you go to your lawyer to prepart your Will.

I hope you enjoy this latest book and that your time in reading it was well spent.

Stephen Paul Tolmie